The Nightshift

By

Jay Darkmoore

Copyright
Jay Darkmoore 2022

All rights reserved. No part of this publication may be reproduced, stored in a retrieval system, or transmitted in an form or by any means without the written permission of the copyright owner.

The Nightshift, taken from the collection of horror stories 'Tales from The Inferno Volume 2' by Jay Darkmoore. If you enjoy this story, you'll love the nightmarish tales of the full book.

To all those things that go bump in the night.
Thank you for the nightmares and inspiration.

Support the author by joining his free reading list –
www.jaydarkmooreauthor.com

Also by Jay Darkmoore –

Horror

The Space Between Heaven and Hell
The Space Between Heaven and Hell – The Shadow Man
Tales From the Inferno Volume One
Tales From the Inferno Volume Two

Dark Fantasy

The Everlife Chronicles – Hunted
The Everlife Chronicles – Conquest
The Everlife Chronicles – Ruin (Coming Soon)

Novellas

Lorna – A Dark Romance

Crime

Detective Laura Warburton – Book One – Left For Dead

From the author –

Back in 2010, I spent a short time living in an old terrace house in my town of Wigan. I always had the feeling of eyes on me, heard noises and had doors close when I left them open. One night, I heard the sound of a woman scream and race up the stairs. I woke up and found the house to be empty and the bedroom next to mines door closed when I had left it open. Inside the room, all the wardrobe doors were open and the once neatly made bed covers were on the floor. I later found out that a previous occupant, a young woman, had hung herself in that same room.

I left that house that night and never went back, but I will hear the scream of that dead woman for the rest of my life.

- Jay Darkmoore

The Nightshift

1
Welcome to Welch Mill

"Have you ever seen a man die?" Carl said, a rugged faced man with skin darker than the coffee he was drinking. His eyes were bulging, veiny like he had forgotten what sleep felt like.

"On the rigs," Tom said, touching the cuffs of his moth bitten suit jacket. "He was a friend of mine. It's the reason I left. Made me think about the dangers of being out on the sea." Tom leant back in his chair, the smell of saltwater tingling his nostrils, then the smell of the extra strong coffee permeating the small office.

"I see," Carl said in his rasping voice. The interview had been going on for just over fifteen minutes, and neither man had said very much at all. Long stares, like Carl, were trying to weigh Tom up, figure him out. See what he was made of. "You ever done security work before Mr. Mackenzie?" Tom shook his head.

"No," he said, a little too quickly. "But," he rebuked, remembering he couldn't afford to fuck up the job opportunity. He had medical bills to pay. "But it can't be that hard, can it?" Again, Tom slapped himself mentally, digging himself an even bigger hole he was trying to claw out of. Carl leaned back and layered those tobacco-stained fingers within each other. His suit jacket was clean, crisp, tailored even.

"It's okay," Carl smiled, his missing teeth pushing through those dry lips like missing tombstones in a graveyard. "Most people say that. The work is easy yes, but the solitude is something you have to be wary of. It's not something to be snuffed at. Long nights alone can play tricks on a man's mind. You're the fifth person I have interviewed for this position in the last six months." Tom raised a brow.

"Why so many?" Carl held his stare. Something was lingering behind those bulging eyes, like a poker player not wanting to let it slip after going all in. But what cards was he holding? Was it a single three or a full house? Tom shook away the feeling of ice creeping under his skin. "I'll be okay. I'm used to being on my own. I'm not scared of the dark." He laughed, but the jovial tone fell dead. Carl's eyes stayed unmoved and his lips remained pursed together.

"I asked you if you have ever seen someone die," Carl said with a heavy tone. Tom again felt the cold return. The touch of the arctic wind on his face carried the screams of a drowning man. He pulled open a drawer and took out some paperwork. "We have spoken to your last employer, Atlantic Oil LTD. They say you had a drinking problem on the rig?"

"I don't know what that has to do with anything?" Tom said, leaning back once more, his hands folding together.

"Is it still a problem?" Carl inquired. Tom's face contorted; his lips tight behind his bushy beard.

"I haven't touched a drop in just under a year." Carl nodded.

"The reason I bring it up Mr. Mackenzie," Carl leaned forward, clearing his throat. "The Night," he said, "The shadows. They can bring things from your mind back to life. Have you ever spoken to a professional about what happened on the rig?" Tom scrunched his face like biting into a rotten apple.

"With all due respect sir, that's none of your business."

"My apologies" Carl rasped, leaning back into his chair again. "The reason I ask is we have had past workers fall under great stress whilst on the shifts. We are a long way from another town and is very solitary. Now you'll be starting this job in the darkest part of the year, not to mention the coldest. I just need to know you're up for the task."

"I can handle it," Tom said. Carl smirked again, that toothy grin peering at him. "What do you mean *great stress?*" Tom asked, more thinking out loud than expecting a real answer. Carl shifted in his seat.

"They have reported strange goings-on. I don't believe in any of it of course, but then again, you are the fifth person I have interviewed for this position in a few months. The last employee was found by the morning cleaner with his hand down to his elbow in the mail sorter. He died en route to the hospital." Tom's eyes widened.

"He lose his fuckin keys or something?" Carl laughed quietly.

"Perhaps." Tom let the story fade from his mind. This was obviously some kind of practical joke they play. He had worked on an oil rig where all people did was scare each other and play jokes on each other all the time. It was the boredom. Play games or go crazy.

Or drink. And drink a lot.

"I'm just making sure your welfare is in check," Carl said.

"Thanks," Tom sighed. "But I'll be fine." Carl nodded and took out some paperwork.

"I don't mean to scare you."

"You can't scare me."

A thick silence fell between the men then. The ticking clock in the corner of the room irking Tom's patience. The large window from the main office next to him was showing lots of cars leaving the parking lot of the warehouse of the Welch Mill Delivery Company. The sun lazily dipped behind the forest that encroached across the road. The streets were going to be busy soon, and he didn't have time to listen to ghost stories. "Sorry to be rude," Tom said, shifting in his chair. "But I have somewhere to be soon. Somewhere important. Have I got the job or not?" Carl took another long drink of his coffee. He checked the clock behind Tom and checked the long shadows creeping from the woods onto the asphalt. He stood, stretching out like a stiff piece of wood and moved to the window. The sun painted the sky pink and red, bleeding into each other as the daylight died. Carl stood silently for a few moments, touching his face and running his hand through his short greying hair. He mustn't have been much older than Tom, maybe mid-fifties, but his face was aged. Deep wrinkles on his neck and cheeks. Finally, at the end of Tom's patience, Carl moved to his desk and took out a small bundle of papers with a pen and pushed them to Tom who began filling them out roughly, signing where the little paper arrows told him to. He handed the paperwork back to him and they shook hands.

"You start tomorrow night," Carl said. Tom nodded a slight smile and began putting on his coat over the faded suit jacket. Carl thumbed the paperwork, a faraway look in his eyes. He took one last look at Tom as he went for the door like he was saying farewell to a man heading off to war. A man whose memory would haunt his dreams forever.

2
Later.

The traffic heading into the city was anything but ideal. As Tom eyed the rows and rows of solid red brake lights in front of him, he felt his blood pressure begin to rise. He turned on the radio of his pick up and let the sound of classic rock pelt his ears for a few moments, before plugging his phone into the centre console and clicking open his music library. A hit of the shuffle button and the melodic sounds of Indie music came flooding into his ears. His mood felt that little bit better, albeit the taunting digital clock on the dashboard flickered at him, telling him he was very late indeed.

The interview had gone well, but Tom felt a little uneasy about it. Not the stories which the manager had told him, he was used to horror stories and things that go bump in the night. You don't spend eight months isolated from the world on an Arctic rig and not see a few strange things after all. Tom saw the phone buzzing and connected it to his Bluetooth. He already had nine points on his driver's license for speeding to late appointments. He didn't need any more for being on his mobile phone, which is why Jayne had bought him the adaptor for the damn thing in the first place.

"I'd rather you get here late than never," she had said one day when he had been pulled over by the police for doing 57 in a 30. Thankfully the officer had a heart and let him off with a warning when Tom explained *'Why he was going so fast, Sir."* Most of his points had come from static speed cameras he hadn't noticed since moving in the area. The heartless robotic fuckers. He answered the phone, swiping along with the screen with his fingertip.

"Hey babe," Tom said, the frustration in his heart-melting away at the sight of her name.

"Hey," she sounded calm which was always a good thing. Happy to speak to him, which was even better. "How did it go?"

"I got the job," Tom said, a little more flatly than would be expected.

"That's great!" Jayne spoke with what little strength she could muster. "How do you feel about it?"

"Happy."

"You don't sound too happy about it?" She said, a little worried.

"You know why Jayne. You know I don't like this kind of work anymore. The only reason I'm taking it is the money is okay, they aren't too strict on the background checks either, and I can start quickly. Didn't even mention my record."

"That's good," she said. "It was a long time ago anyway."

"I know," he said. "The interviewer was a real stiff though!" Tom let his hard lips crack a smile. Jayne giggled. He imagined her standing against the wall, cradling the phone in her ear and twiddling the cable around her fingertips. But he knew she would still be in her bed, the credit on the call soon to run out.

"Oh really? I can't wait to see you and you tell me about it!" She laughed again, and that sweet sound cut Tom into pieces. He ran his rough tongue along his lips, his beard leaving a taste of tobacco in his mouth that had stained his facial hair a dirty yellow. He hadn't smoked since Jayne had come home from the doctors, but that craving had never left him. He just got better at ignoring it.

"I don't have to take the job you know," Tom said with a sigh. "I would rather stay at home and take care of you myself. We can take the hit on the money. We can live off what I got from the Rig. We can…" Jayne cut him off.

"Don't be saying things like that Sash." *Sash.* He hated that nickname but she loved it. *"Sasquatch" Aka Big hairy bastard.* "You were going nuts being at home with me, and the carers help so much. We can't just 'survive' off the little money we have left. I wouldn't want that for you, or for me. I feel like a burden enough." The traffic began to move, but Tom was focused on the feeling of his throat being sewed up. A blaring horn snapped his attention back to the road and he waved to the animated prick in a Porsche behind him. "You aren't a burden baby." A small silence then. "How're you feeling today?"

"Oh, you know me, I keep going." He could tell she was smiling, and again, his throat sewed shut that little tighter. "The job will be good for you."

"I don't want it, Jayne. I don't do well for long periods of time in the night. Messes with my head." The two went quiet again. Then she spoke.

"I know Sash. Since what happened with Brad, I..." *Brad.* The name cut through him.

"Sorry I have to go," he said bluntly. "I'll be there soon." Tom hung up the phone. He didn't need to think about that. He didn't need to think about the sound of screams in the midnight sea. He was reminded of them enough.

3
Evening.

He pulled up to their house and let the engine idle a few moments so the heating stayed on. It was winter, and the snow was due to fall any day now, and the bite of the wind was a constant reminder that the hot summer and picnics in the park were a faded memory. The large trees that lined their street, once so vibrant and green and teeming with birds and squirrels and all kinds of other critters, were now stripped and barren, like lonely skeletons standing by the roadside, trying to lean down and touch those living underneath it with its wooden fingertips. He pushed the door open and brought in Jayne's bags and placed them in the living room next to her bed. He put the fire on, lighting it with a couple of matches and then put it on a low setting whilst the logs burned and popped in a growing glow of red, like pulsing veins of lava pushing through the wood giving way to thousands of tiny dancers dressed in blue and yellow.

Back outside, Jayne sat bundled up in her coat with her scarf around her head. She had asked the nurse to draw her eyebrows on for her, which Tom thought to be strange. He thought a moment of rubbing them off and redoing them, making her look constantly surprised, but he didn't think that would be appropriate. He opened the door, trying to shield Jayne as much as possible from the cold breeze.

The sun had fully dropped below the horizon now, painting the sky in dark reds and yellows, bleeding away from a dull blue. The moon in its full phase, looking over them. Tom eyed the skyline as he carried Jayne into the house. It reminded him of those long nights at sea, where the night sky was bursting with billions of tiny lights like a black canvas left in the hands of a toddler armed with glitter and glue.

He got her in and carried her onto the bed. Undressing her, he wiped her down with wet wipes and redressed her in her nightgown. She had been sleeping most of the journey back home, and even him carrying her didn't wake her fully. She stirred a little and cracked him a small smile, but then sleep took her once more. He tucked her in the metal-framed bed, and got her bedpan and her crutches next to the railings should she need to get out for some reason. He fluffed her pillows and put some lavender oil on the duvet. She always loved the smell of lavender. That, and roses, but he was fresh out of that one. Finally, he placed her slippers over her feet and tucked them under the covers, and hooked up the IV drip and the heart monitors to her. She looked a little like a robot; wires poking out here, there and everywhere, and the sight of her made his stone face begin to weep. He never cried when she was awake. He wouldn't let her see him like that, so he bottled it up for moments like this when he could allow himself to grieve for his wife that still breathed. Only a few tears though, never anything more than that. He couldn't open the dam fully or he might not be able to close it again. Carl's voice pushed into his mind.

"The shadows. They can bring things from your mind back to life. Have you ever spoken to a professional about what happened?" Tom shook the sound of him away and stuck something on the TV. He listened quietly to the sound of the heart monitor beeping and took out his journal from the side of the bed. He had always written down his thoughts. Something that helped him get through the months at sea. Something that stopped him diving in it at times too.

Sunday 22:03

Home

Jayne is in bed now. I'm glad she didn't have too much of a bad time at the hospital. She's such a strong woman. God knows I would be telling everyone how much that fucking camera hurt. There must be a better way of finding tumours in the stomach, right? Rather than a damn camera?

The chemo is kicking her ass. She hasn't been sick much, but her hair has finally gone, and she is so weak and sleeps most of the time.

She wants me to go for this job. I don't want too really; I want to stay with her. What if something happens and I'm not here? I know her sister is only a few minutes away, but still.

She does want me to get out of the house though. And to be honest, the break would be nice.

Tom looked at this last line. "The break would be nice?" He scalded himself, almost disgusted at what he had written. He tore the page out and threw it on the fire. He called himself a prick and wrote something new –

Sunday 22:09
Home

I got the job. Jayne's doing as well as she can. Some shit on Tv. I could kill for a drink. Goodnight.
- Sash

4
Welcome To Welch Mill

"Coffee machine is busted," Jerry said, his unbuttoned shirt giving way to his flabby neck. Tom looked at him with amazement. There was no way someone as 'big-boned,' as Jerry should be wearing a shirt that tight. Let alone walking around the warehouse on the night shift.

"Got it," Tom said, looking at the broken machine.

"So, if you want some, you'll have to bring your own."

"Gotcha," Tom laughed, remembering the pack of supplies in his car.

"I'm sure I will," Tom eyed up the cupboards, seeing if he could salvage a beverage, courtesy of the company. He began pulling doors open, looking through the tea-stained cupboards in the warehouse canteen. He pulled old cardboard boxes out of different styled tea bags. Most of them are empty: regular, extra strong. The De Caff teabags were still in their plastic wrapping, and Tom wasn't that desperate yet. His fingers reached all the way to the back and he pulled out a small box of green tea. He gave them a glance and took one out, then flipped on the kettle that looked more used than a £5 whore in Amsterdam. Jerry eyed the green tea bag sitting in the cup. Tom sensed the glare. "What?" He said, a little more defensively than he intended. He didn't want to come off as a dick on his first job. Especially not to his new boss.

"Nothing," Jerry said. "The last guy we had doing the night watch security shift was into the herbal stuff too. He was a little…" Jerry made a circle with his finger around his temple. "Squirrely." Tom tried to hold back the smile beginning to crack behind his thick brown beard. Jerry's face stayed stoic and flat, so Tom buried the smirk behind the bush of tight whiskers.

"Squirrely?" He said.

"Yeah." Jerry nodded. "But, working a shift like this? Alone in your post watching the monitors? It can get to a person sometimes."

"Really?" Tom said. His skin beginning to flush. He thought again about the bullshit interview he had the day before. How they were trying to pull his leg. It seemed everyone was in on the gag. "How so?" Jerry went to speak, his large belly rising as he struggled to take in a full breath. The man must have easily weighed close to thirty stone, and if Tom smelt as bad as he did, he wouldn't want to take a breath too deep either.

"Well, you're the fifth guy we've had in the past few months doing this work. I don't get it," Jerry said. "The money is decent, the hours are long, yeah, but you get the radio, the canteen and get to relax. Just, for some reason, no one seems to want to stay very long. It's annoying actually. Finding new staff all the time." Tom felt the room grow a little warmer.

"Why does nobody seem to want the job? Is it the isolation? I worked away for years on the oil rigs in the Atlantic. My own company is what I prefer. People are arseholes. No disrespect."

"None taken," Jerry said, resting his sausage fingers on the stained counter. "Two guys left without giving notice, and the last guy, the one who liked the herbal tea, was found in a bad way." Tom's ears pricked.

"A bad way?" Tom eyed Jerry who shrugged.

"He was always a little odd. Was found trying to pull something out of Gretta."

"Gretta?"

"The mail feeder," Jerry said. "Big fucking rattling thing in the middle of the warehouse in between the mail racks. Can sort and spit out over one thousand envelopes sizes A4 to A6 in less than a minute," Jerry said almost proudly. "Poor bastard was found by the cleaner in the morning with his arm up to his elbow in the mouth of Gretta. She had almost chewed it off."

"That sounds terrible," Tom said coldly. Jerry shrugged once more. Maybe getting his exercise in for the day.

"He was a weird guy. Was still alive too when the cleaner found him. Taken away in the ambulance. Kept on talking about 'The Night.' Fuck if I know. Guy was a freak. Ex junkie. Been in prison for armed robbery a few years back. Was found with LSD in his bloodstream. Go figure."

"You normally hire ex-cons?" Tom asked.

"Most of the time in fact," Jerry said. "The company is part of some government scheme. We hire those trying to get their shit together, and the government pays seventy-five percent of the wages."

"That's good," Tom said. "What were the others like?"

"The employees? One was an ex-coke dealer, the other, a woman, was into fraud." Tom smiled slightly.

"Giving people a second chance. I like that. But the LSD thing? I knew a guy once that fell into a bush and thought he was time itself. Spent three hours masturbating until the police got hold of him." Both men laughed loudly. "What was the guy's name? The one who decided to feed his arm to Gretta?"

"Fuck if I remember," Jerry snorted. "Wallace? Walter? Willy? We have that many different staff here, nobody can keep track of the new faces." Jerry eyed him and smiled slightly. "Speaking of convictions," Jerry said, eyeing him. Tom felt the room grow a little warmer. "Don't worry about it. I know you've got your shit together," he said, almost condescendingly. Tom went to speak but the kettle clicked off. "Your water is ready," Jerry said, quickly changing the subject, exhaling a steady blow breath smelling of takeaways and cigarettes.

5
Welcome To Welch Mill

They walked from the canteen through the corridor. It wasn't well lit, and the only light coming from a few single lonely bulbs suspended from the ceiling by thick wiring like glow in the dark spiders. Portraits of employees and message boards hung on the walls. Tom noticed a fundraiser was happening for a local cancer charity. *'Race for life.'*

"You got a pen?" Tom said, holding his hand out. Jerry turned with a grunt. He was panting. He must be sweating his back out now in the fifteen feet they've walked from the canteen.

"What?" He said. He looked upon it with horror. "You don't want to go running do you?" He gasped.

"I like being outdoors, doing some exercise. Like I said, I was on the Oil Rigs. Only dead men stay idle."

"True," Jerry said, scratching his large chin, digging his fingers between the acne and patches of unshaven stubble. "Not for me though." *I've noticed,* Tom thought. Jerry studied the board a little closer. His big eyes bulging under his heavy rimmed glasses.

"Well if you want to join, you gotta put your name down." He handed Tom a pen. "It's a good cause though. I usually join them afterwards for a couple of drinks down the pub." Tom wrote his name on the A4 paper underneath the flyer.

"I want to book that night off," Tom said, handing the pen back. Jerry laughed.

"Jesus, not even done your first night and you're making demands. You'll be after my job next." Tom didn't share the big man's laughter. He tapped the date with his pen, holding Jerry's gaze. His smile faded.

"September 8th. I am taking that day off," he said stoically.

"Remind me in the morning, okay? I'll see what I can do for you." The two continued through the corridor. It wasn't very long, maybe a hundred feet or so, and they passed a few offices which still had their monitors on standby with big sticky notes with big black ink saying 'LOG OFF DON'T SWITCH OFF,' in good passive-aggressive office fashion, the screensavers light pushing through the darkened windows. They got to the opening at the end and Jerry pushed open the double doors. Both stepped through and he held out his hand at the large open space in front of him. His face painted in a wide grin under the dull light, like a slave trader telling his new arrivals they were going to work in the land of milk and honey, the look of pride slapped across his face.

"This is *my* baby. *My* creation." Jerry let out a satisfied grin, and Tom half expected him to either burst into tears, break into song, or touch Tom's shoulder with a solemn look in his eye. None of which Tom particularly welcomed.

"It's big," Tom said flatly, looking into the warehouse filled with rows upon rows of shelves of different boxes and bundles of paper. A sleeping forklift truck sat alone in the far corner under a fluorescent light strip which flickered and blinked. Tom eyed the small bar to the left. It was waist height and made of white chipped wood. Behind it, several large panes of glass and a door leading into the room behind. Through the glass, a chair and several monitors propped up. The view of the security stream was visible from where he was standing.

"I'm guessing that's where I'm going to be calling home for the rest of the night?" Tom queried, nodding to his nocturnal palace with his cap.

"Indeed. That's gonna be you." Jerry stood back upright after taking a rest against the wall. "Some more things I gotta show you first." The two men meandered through the warehouse shop floor. Jerry taking pleasure in showing him the alphabetised freight, mail, optics and sorting panels. "This is where the magic really happens," he said, gesturing to a bunch of yellow and white sacks made of rough woven plastic, dangling from metal hooks like dismembered ball sacks. "The sorters get mail from all over the country, and it all comes out of this machine right here." He tapped on a large metal machine with a huge open mouth, baskets and mesh wiring at the bottom, loose letters and documents clinging for dear life on the edge, less they fall onto the ground.

"I'm guessing this is Gretta?" Tom said, inspecting the machine for remnants of bone and fingernails. Jerry nodded.

"You guess correctly. She may look gentle, but she can bite. As well as the last weirdo you're taking over from, we've had another couple of guys lose a finger or two in this thing. One guy mangled his hand up really bad. Nothing a nice redundancy package can't fix though." Jerry slapped Tom's shoulder. Tom's boulder-like shoulders didn't budge, nor did his stern face.

"Was he okay?"

"Of a fashion," he said. "He had to learn to jerk off with the other hand if that makes you feel any better." It didn't make Tom feel any better. Considering the state-of-the-art machinery and set-up of the place, and how reputable the company was, it seemed like a little circus show of horrors. He had been here for less than an hour and already learned of several accidents. Tom wondered how they hadn't been sued or closed down, but he didn't figure he should bring up such things on his first shift. He wondered what else had gone on and why the manager was being so coy about the whole thing.

"This place pays weekly right?" He said as Jerry continued to show him the wonderers of the warehouse.

"It sure does. Or monthly if you prefer."

"Weekly is fine." Tom stopped and sighed. "Look, I'm gonna need a week upfront if that's okay? I hate to ask but, the wife…" Jerry stopped mid-shelf fingering and turned to Tom. Tom stood stoic, trying not to look too desperate. He never asked for money, ever. But a time comes when a man has to swallow his pride and ask for help, and here he was, swallowing it up by the spoonful. "I'm sorry," Tom said after a moment of silence. "I just…"

"No, that's completely okay Tom," Jerry said. "I understand. I'll see what I can do for you." Tom felt his heart beat a little slower. A feeling of warmth rushed through him and for the first time in a while, he felt a blanket of genuine warmth wrap around him, and dare he think, he cracked a smile under those dim lights.

"Thanks, Boss. It'll help a lot."

"You've got a big heart, Tom. I can see that. Nothing wrong with sharing a little kindness. Not enough of that these days." He moved in a little closer and gripped Tom's hand, tightly. "You'll do well here my man." He surveyed the racking and boxes. "Yeah, you'll fit *right* in here."

The two continued to the last part of the warehouse. A small door was set at the back which was locked. It looked as though the room had been thrown up in a haste; the walls were thin and made of plywood. Roughly painted and had no windows. Jerry pulled out a set of keys and unlocked the door. Inside was the loneliest damn toilet Tom had ever seen. The thing looked so cold Tom thought if he went on it for too long the base would strip off the top layer of ass hair and skin. Tom figured he would not be using the shitter tonight. The last thing he wanted was to be sat frozen to the bowl mid shit, unable to run and stop intruders from ransacking the safe in the boss's office. How the hell would he explain *that* mess when he got home?

"I personally like to use this when the place is quiet," Jerry said. "It's small, secluded and is locked. It isn't much, but it's more solitary than the others you'll find near the canteen in the hallway we came through to get here. Most of the workers use it too. Let's face it, no one likes others hearing them shit." The idea wasn't appealing to Tom, like him going to the cheap whore all the guys had already ran through, but he smiled and nodded anyway. Jerry closed the door. "Now, the part you have been waiting for." Jerry began walking, the smell of sweat stinging Tom's nose. "Your office!"

6
Welcome To Welch Mill

The skin around Tom's ball sack tightened and his breath pushed from his mouth in a puff of smoke. He zipped up his thick jacket uptight and dipped his cap down. He was thankful he wore extra layers before coming out, the winter air biting his skin.

"Cold?" Jerry said, hulking his huge feet along the ground.

"Freezing."

"You get used to it. Trust me." *Easy for you to say walking around with all that blubber.*

"Don't you have the heating on or anything?" Tom asked, pressing his beard down into his neck. Jerry shook his head.

"Sorry kid." Tom's nostrils flared. *Kid. Don't call me a fucking kid.* "Thermostat's been busted for a little while. Just in time for December. Merry Christmas to us hey? There's a small heater in your security room. Nothing fancy, but should stop the icicles from forming in your nostrils." They walked around the wooden bar and through a singular door in between the large glass panes. Tom saw filing cabinets lining the walls, an old ticking clock that seemed to be busted, to his delight. A couple of desks with dead monitors, reflecting his etched ghostly silhouette back at him. On one of the desks bore a small placard that read 'YOU DON'T NEED TO BE MAD TO WORK HERE, BUT IT HELPS!' and another, more macabre one 'LEAVE YOUR SOUL AT THE DOOR. YOU WON'T NEED IT HERE.' How to sell a place to a guy. At the back of the office stood another door, brown and looking like it wouldn't hold back a pissed-off mouse, let alone an intruder, with the word 'SEC RITY' written on the front. The 'U' was missing.

"Where's the rest of the sign?" Tom pointed out. Jerry, who had pulled out a bar of chocolate from fuck knows where, studied the sign under the harsh UV strip lighting. He shrugged.

"No 'U'. I suppose the 'U' isn't important. As long as someone sits in that room and watches the monitors, it doesn't matter what the sign reads." Tom felt a little offended like he wasn't needed. But he had a point. It could have easily read 'Secretary,' which he supposed when there's nobody home and he's the only one there, it's pretty much the same thing.

His mind wandered back to Jayne. She had been a secretary in her old job before she had gotten too sick. Tom had finished at the rig and was working as a mechanic. The hours were long and he was often exhausted when he got home and stinking of motor oil. Jayne's doctors had said it was just fatigue, stress, and maybe even a little bit of the flu. But when the 'flu' got didn't go away, it turned out to be much worse, and Tom hung up his tools to be at home for her in the daytime hours. He didn't need sleep. He never had. A couple of hours and a power nap through the day had been what he was used to when working those long months out at sea. His doctor said he was heading towards a heart attack through stress and his nervous system was at risk of burning out. But he never listened to the advice of the doctors. Jayne's illness was a prime example, but it started earlier than that from how his mother had believed in them so avidly. Until a Tuesday afternoon check-up turned into something sinister growing inside of her, missed over and over, until she vanished into herself, Gin her new best friend.

He shook the memory of his mother from his mind. Why had she popped into his head? He hadn't thought of her in months, longer even. God, had it been *that* long? It must have been close to five years this coming Christmas, when she sank half a bottle of *Gordons Dry* and got behind the wheel of her car –

"Are you listening?" Jerry scowled.

"Yeah," Tom hurried, scratching the back of his head, letting the memory of mangled metal and broken headlights fade from his mind. Jerry eyed him with those reddening eyes and those puffy sacks hanging underneath them. He gestured to the single chair propped up against a wooden desk with three monitors with split screens in front of it. They were black and white, except for the canteen which was in colour, the lights still on.

"This is the epicenter of security of my warehouse," he enunciated the last part like he was speaking about a prized possession, a child, a lover or the last bag of Doritos. "Here," he made a sweeping motion with his hands, like he had discovered the lost treasure of Horus in the Valley of Kings, "is where you will spend your shift, looking over these monitors with explicit attention. Anything moves, you check it out. There's a flashlight in the drawer with a ton of batteries, and there's a kettle and sink over there," he pointed to a small fridge and washbasin. "We don't keep it stocked though, so I imagine you brought your own things?"

"I did. It's in my car out back. I'll get my bag before you leave."

"Wonderful news. Don't want you falling asleep on me. Gotta keep my baby in check."

"Yes Sir," Tom said bluntly.

"Sir was my dad and he was a prick. Call me Jerry." He said, puffing out his chest.

"Thanks," Tom said sourly, "but I prefer Sir. I think familiarity breeds contentment, and I'm not into letting myself get too close. No offence." Jerry was taken back. He obviously wasn't used to being told *no*.

"I see. Any reason for that?" Jerry waited for an answer. Tom took in a breath. He heard the swooping of waves and thunder. The wild air against his hair and the calls of a drowning man in the black tirading sea.

"Experience."

7
The Shadow on the Monitor

Tom walked alone out of the SEC RITY office and through the warehouse. He meandered down the hallways past the empty offices of Payroll, Human Resources, Witch Craft, and into the main lobby, where customers came to collect missed parcels, mail, lost children, and pressed his lanyard against the small black box at the entrance and pushed open the set of double glass doors. The night air hit him like a truck, and he could see the night sky suffocated by black clouds, the last remnants of the evening sun disappearing behind a snaking black claw in the night sky. Considering he had the cloud coverage, the night air bit his balls worse than foreplay gone wrong. He walked along the walkway lined with dull grass, the sound of his boots clicking on the asphalt. He reached his numbing fingers into his pocket and pulled out his car keys for his truck. He clicked the button and the machine's headlights lit up.

Hello again. That was a quick shift? Did you miss me?

The sound of his wife in his ear. He shook her away. He didn't need any distractions right now. The first night away from her, leaving her alone in bed, against all his morality. But when you have wolves knocking at your door asking for bills to be paid and there's no more 'Just one more month' chances left, you gotta ignore the pain in your chest and do what makes sense. Tom pulled at the door handle and the gathering frost crunched, relinquishing its icy grip before popping open where he climbed into the driver's seat.

"Don't feel bad," Jayne had said as he was leaving earlier that night. "I know you don't want to go, but you're going crazy being at home with me all the time. You'll be fine, and so will I. If I need anything, I can call *my sister. You get out for a while and enjoy the first shift at the new job. You'll love it. You need it. I love you."*

He bit down on his lip hard, trying to stop the rawness creeping in. He slammed his hand on the steering wheel and gripped it tightly, pressing his head into the leather. He breathed long and hard, remembering what his councilor had said. *Breathe, and breathe a little more until it passes.* So he did just that, and after a few moments, the pain subsided, the thought of his wife being without him, or more likely, him being without her.

He reached in and took out his rucksack from the passenger seat. It was filled with snacks, a metal flask of coffee and a couple of tea bags and a bottle of milk just to be safe. He had his journal too, to make notes of interesting things he would see on the cameras. Conversation topics for when he got home. God knows they needed something new to talk about *other* than the Cancer. He threw the bag over his shoulder and shut the door. He checked for his mobile phone and battery pack, fingers pushing past the packet of biscuits and chicken bites, he found it there tucked at the bottom and breathed a sigh of relief, a plume of ghostly smoke clinging to the inside of the windshield.

Tom walked back to the entrance of the building. It stood in front of his home for the night, taking it all in as the night air numbed his face. The building was big and made of iron cladding, like a mountain of black obscuring anything and everything the closer you got to it. Thankfully it was only one story. There was the lower deck, which you needed to take a ride in a rickety elevator to get to, but that was where the uncollected parcels without a return address were kept. After six months they were either destroyed or if it was something good, auctioned off at the annual Christmas party. He's been told by Jerry that someone got a Rolex last year. Work all year in a job you hate for the chance of something good at the end. And people called *him* crazy for picking the night shift. The money wasn't terrible however, so he convinced himself anyway. It was a little over minimum wage, but the option for overtime was always there, and the work wasn't hard. Watch a bunch of monitors for a few hours, read a book, and watch a movie. How hard could it be? He felt the baseball bat in his carryall digging into his shoulder. *Just in case,* He thought, and the feel of that metallic hitting stick made him feel that little bit safer. He took out his lanyard as he got to the front entrance. It was wrapped awkwardly around his neck and arm, so he dropped the rucksack to the ground to stop him from garroting himself as he took out his pass.

He heard footsteps quickly behind him. He spun around on the spot, his heart jackhammering. Nothing in the darkness moved, the night air seeming a little warmer as his face started to flush with blood. He didn't call out to the darkness. Only fucking morons did that. He'd seen his share of horror movies, and he wasn't in the habit of walking into the woods alone because he heard something moving. He waited a moment. Something moved in the distance in the tree line behind the car park. It was small, dimly lit by the street lighting of the car park. A moment later, he saw it emerge from the distance.

A dog.

Tom meandered back to the SEC RITY room where he found Jerry looking over the monitors.

"Do you see it?" Tom asked, gesturing to the screens. Jerry moved next to him, his heavyweight creaking the table.

"See what?"

"The dog on the monitor, in the distance. Little thing. Thin too." Jerry eyed the screens again. He shook his head.

"No," he said, "I don't see anything." Tom queried the big man.

"You sure? It was right there." Tom pointed to where the dog had been. Jerry again looked at him for longer than was comfortable.

"You probably did see one," he said. "We get them from time to time, all sorts actually: badgers, deer, foxes. All kinds of critters. If they come to the building, do me a favour and don't feed them.

You'll end up like the last guy, screaming to high hell about the damn dogs he kept feeding on shift."

"Like the last guy?" Tom scrunched his face a little. "You mean Wallace?"

"Something like that." Jerry scratched his receding hairline. "The guy was seen coming into work in his last few shifts with bags and bags of fresh meat for the damn things. He was warned about it a few times." He put a sausage finger on the monitor. "They're fucking huge those woods. Go on for miles in all sorts of directions. All sorts of things goings on in there." Jerry pulled out a bundle of papers in a binder and began flicking through them on the desk. Tom wanted to pry further but held his tongue. Didn't want him thinking he was turning squirrely on his first night.

The two went over some more of the checks, the HR Policy and the fire evacuation procedure. Who to call if the cameras go off? Who *not* to call should anything else go wrong? "I have had the pleasure of being on call for your first week. Carl, the guy who interviewed you, doesn't like to be pestered every five minutes by the newbies. I'm not happy about it, but I get paid for it. Anything you need to ask about: questions, queries, where the toilet paper is kept, give me a call." He looked up from the bundle of paperwork and gave a slight smile. "But don't take the piss."

"I'll be fine Sir."

"Wonderful." Jerry packed the papers up. "I'll see you in the morning. Have a good shift."

8
The First Night

Monday 21:30

SEC RITY ROOM

I honestly thought I thought I was going to throw up at the smell of that fat bastard's body odour. I mean, I don't shower every day or use deodorant all the time, but Jesus, that guy needs Febreze lined clothing.

Anyway. First night is underway. Got the game on my phone. England are winning, which is surprising. Thankfully I remembered my charger, because it would have been a long night otherwise. The monitors are pretty quiet at the moment. I saw a dog too. It was a skinny thing, maybe a Rottie or something, but still I saw it sniffing around the truck. Maybe I dropped something on my way in. It had gone by the time Jerry had come around though. Little bugger probably took a quick shit and ran away. I'll have to watch my step when I leave in the morning. Place is a little cold but nothing I can't handle. But I gotta remember to bring some extra layers with the weather set to change.

I keep thinking about you, babe. I'm watching the clock and trying to resist the urge to call you and check-in. I know you'll be alright. It's just a few hours and I'll be home again to make you some breakfast.

I did hear something strange before though, and to be honest, I don't really want to write it down, but I will anyway so we can talk about it when I get home. I could have sworn when I was getting out of my car and walking to the building earlier, that I heard footsteps behind me. I turned around, ready to beat the fuck out of some little punk who thought I'd be an easy target, but only the wind met me. The wind, and the trees in the distance. Either I imagined it, or they have some big fucking squirrels around here.

He put the pen down and giggled at the thought of a squirrel running around the car park in a pair of size twelve steel toe capped boots. He sat back and watched England play the last few minutes of the game against Switzerland from the iPlayer. He hadn't watched it as he needed some sleep earlier in the day, and had avoided all social media, not like he went on much anyway, to not risk seeing the result. They were winning one-nil so far, and a few moments later, as Tom had cracked open his Thermos and poured himself a cup of coffee, the game ended and Tom turned it off and put the phone on standby mode, before checking if he had any missed calls. He saw there were none, and checked his voicemail just to be sure, before putting it away in his jacket pocket.

Tom had experienced the quiet before when he was out at sea. He had been in the middle of nowhere: no wind, no stars and just the slightest lick of the gentle sea touching the foundations of the rig. But as he sat there in his chair, coffee in hand, he could hear the sound of his heart beating in his ears. He looked over the monitors, the grey static picture looking back at him. Tom remembered something else he wanted to write in the journal, to say something about the game. He pulled it open and got to work.

Also,

The game was pretty good, E gla d play we

"Fuck," he hissed as the pen ran out of ink. He hoped he had brought another one and rummaged through his bag to fish another biro or hell, a damn pencil would do. He fingered through the bottom past the array of snacks and goodies he had with him, but there was no pen. He wasn't desperate enough to write about England not playing terrible to use a sachet of tomato sauce, however the thought did cross his mind. Instead, he sat back and looked around the desk for something to write with. He cracked open the drawer on the cabinet and smiled. To his heart's content, there was a nice crisp biro in black to write down his thoughts. He picked it up and went to write. As he closed the drawer, the pen slipped from his fingers and he crouched to get it. He mustn't have been concentrating, because he lifted his head and banged it on the bottom of the protruding drawer, a small cut appearing at the top of his skull. He bit down and hissed, then let out a long, seething "Motherfucker," before leaning back in the chair. Tom leant to close the drawer when he saw his colossal head had dislodged the bottom. Again, he called himself a fucking idiot, knowing this would no doubt come out of his paycheque, but as he looked further, he saw something-

The drawer had a false bottom, and under it was what looked to be a small stack of papers. Tom put his hand in and fished out the bundle. It was coated in a light dust, and he blew on it, sending particles across the monitors. The wedges were frayed and browned, and the spine of the book was well worn.

"The Space Between," he mouthed the name of the story. The cover was like the old readers' digest books you could order. No picture, just a leather dust jacket with the title on the front. No author either. Tom opened it, the smell of damp and mothballs pushing into his nostrils.

"As I wandered through the howling night under the midnight sun, I found myself in a precarious position. One not of contemptment, but of fear. A primal fear that one doesn't inherently understand, but is all too familiar when its icy fingernails trace up your spine.

"Alone I wander through this wood. Dark and void of life. Like the winter hath stripped all its delights and warmth, leaving only a skeleton of its former self. A shell, if you will. A shell of its former glory."

What Tom could surmise; it was the story of a boy who had lost his friend in a large forest. Either lost, or he had been abandoned and was trying to find his way home. It was macabre at best. He put the book down a moment and gave a quick look over the monitors. All still on that black and white screen. He flicked through the cameras: the basement, the offices, the warehouse and then finally the car park. Nothing of note.

Tom dug into his duffel bag and pulled out a couple of small snacks. More out of boredom than hunger, and dug into some biscuits.   He opened up his journal, touching the cut at the top of his head. He wouldn't need stitches, but the morning shower would hurt like a bitch. He moved over to a fresh page, after crossing out the shit about England playing well. *Not meant to be* boys he thought to himself with a small smile. He took out a pack of Nicotine gum from his pocket and started to chew.

He held his hand steady a moment, unable to bring himself to mark it. The blank page eyeing him like it had teeth. His pen hesitated over the first line, like about to step into freshly laid snow. You want the first imprint to be good, and he didn't want to fuck it up on the first word. *How the hell do writers do this?* He thought to himself, thinking of all the books he had read, amazed how they all started out as empty space.

Only a few hours in. Not long left to go now.

P.S. I hit my head. It fucking hurt, but I found a book which I might give a read. Seems to have been written by some pretentious bastard, but I don't know why it was there? Maybe one of the old workers had left it there. Maybe it's actually filled with nude pictures and it was his hiding place for them?

He put the pen down. That would do for now. He would come back to it when he thought of something else to say to himself, or more, to make notes to tell Jayne later.

9
Dawn

"How was the first night?" Jerry said, opening the door at 7 am sharp. Tom was a little further into the book he found, so engrossed in it that he didn't hear the big man come in. The boss eyed him annoyed. "You should be watching the monitors, not a book." Again, Tom didn't stir, staring at the book, like he was sleeping with his eyes open. Jerry moved to him, half wondering if he was dead with his eyes open. He looked over his shoulder to see if there were some nudie photos hidden in there which Tom didn't feel like sharing. "What you got there?" He said, moving closer. Tom could feel the breath on his neck, but he still didn't pull his attention from the pages, his knuckles turning white, digging into the leather cover. Jerry's eyes licked the pages, and his heart skipped a beat. "Hey!" He bolstered, kicking the chair Tom was in. Tom flinched, rubbing his eyes, breathing quickly like he had been shocked by a raw wire when putting up the Christmas tree.

"Hey boss," he said, running his hand through his hair and beard. "You been there long?"

The drive home was as shit as you could imagine. The first night shift, the busy roads that kept you from your bed, and the fumes you were running on, trying to stay awake before the copious amounts of caffeine in your system began to drop. A red light, then another red light. Tom beeped his horn at a slow motorist and revved the beast's engine loudly, digging the needle into the red. The car in front waved him a *fuck you* then took off. Tom continued quickly behind it, before turning off the junction before the motorway. He didn't need to go on that in rush hour, so he took the longer route. It would be faster, less well known. He never used a sat nav, he found them to be lazy. So many people got caught in unnecessary traffic because they relied on a computer to tell them where to go. Tom however knew this part of town like the back of his hand; the back routes always got him where he needed to be without being stuck behind Miss fucking Daisy.

He got onto the long stretch of dirt road that ran parallel to the motorway where he could see hundreds of parked cars. The morning was still pretty dark, so the motorway looked like a million red eyes blaring into the morning twilight. Tom pulled out his phone and quickly checked if there were any missed calls. Nothing. No messages either. He checked the road in front of him, cruising with one hand on the wheel, his attention elsewhere. He punched in the number for his voicemail and looked up, raising the phone to his ear.

A dog! A fucking dog!

Tom stomped on the brakes of the beast as hard as he could, sending his mobile flying along the ground and slamming into the side of the passenger door footwell. The back end of the beast slid as the wheels locked, the dashboard lighting up with the ABS sensor, the brakes releasing and tightening quicker than a virgin's first orgasm. The dog in his headlights didn't move, it only stood there as the giant hunk of metal corralled towards it. Tom bit down, his arms straight, his body tight, twisting the steering wheel, banking a hard right to the wrong side of the road, just narrowly missing the animal. The engine began to stall, heading straight for a farmer's brick wall that lined a huge empty field filled with low mist. He slammed his foot on the clutch, threw the beast into first and pulled the clutch back up and revved the engine, forcing the rev counter right into the red for the second time that morning, the hood of the pick-up stopping inches from the brick wall. Tom held his gaze on the wall lit up by the bright lights for a second, panting heavily. Once he caught his breath and was sure he hadn't shit himself, he looked in the rear-view mirror. The dog was gone.

He arrived home around twenty minutes later, his feet crunching on the fallen snow as he made his way to the front door. The lights were still off which was a good thing. It meant that Jayne hadn't been getting up during the night, or if she had, she had been strong enough to turn the lights on and off. Tom put his key in the lock and stepped inside. The house was quiet, the small sound of the television set still on in the background. The smell of the gas fire in the air, the heat making the home a cosy little number. He stepped into the living room, knocking the snow from his boots which gathered on his heels. Jayne was still in bed sleeping soundly. He moved quietly and kissed her on the top of her head, running his fingers over the smoothness. He eyed her a moment, his heart catching in his throat. No matter how many times he saw her, she looked so beautiful, even though the illness was slowly eating her alive. The chemo was helping, and they had seen a lot of progress and regression of the cancer, but that didn't mean her clothes fit well. She hadn't eaten a substantial meal in months, surviving on bits of soup and when she could stomach it, a slice of bread or two. Tom had lost weight too as a result. No point making a huge meal when there's only him to eat it. He changed her bedpan and got her morning medication ready with a drink of water next to her bed for when she woke up.

Tom kicked off his boots and lay his head down on the couch next to her, flicking through the tv channels with no real interest. He couldn't wait to see his wife open her eyes again so they could talk about what had happened on his shift, or lack of. The heat from the gas fire continued to swell and grow, melting the frost that gathered around his beard, his head nestling into the cushions before his heavy eyes finally closed.

Pans and cutlery rattled around him. Tom opened his eyes lazily. It was still dark. Had he slept all day? Panic struck him. He needed to feed Jayne, give her medication. He sat up and saw her bed to be empty. His stomach felt like it had been plunged into an icy river. He got to his feet. He stumbled. He was woozy. Was he drunk? No, he hadn't touched the stuff since the oil rigs. Since Brad. The room was a blanket of darkness. The kitchen door was closed, only a band of golden light pushing through the darkness that encased him. Tom pushed the door open. "Jayne?" He whispered. "Is that you?"

The door opened and Tom felt the splash of seawater on his skin. The icy wind ripped through him and he closed his thick high vis jacket around him, zipping it up as fast as his thick cumbersome gloves would allow him. The tirading black sea smashed against the rig, huge waves of the abyss slamming and soaking him in a drenching downpour. The lights of the rig were flashing red, and Tom knew what that meant.

Man Overboard!

Tom raced, still falling over his own feet, the smell of whisky on his breath. The hard steel flooring digging into his knees and into his elbows as he crawled. He gripped the railings and eyed the scurrying men below him on the lower deck, pointing search lights into the never-ending sea. A flash of high vis in the water before it vanished again below the surface. Men and women throwing buoys and life rings out as far as they could, trying to command the flailing body in the water to grab hold.

Tom bolted awake, his arms flailing like he was sinking below the surface of dark water. Tom's face slapped with worry, sweating and panting. He was drenched. He hadn't taken his coat off from outside and he was lying in a pool of his own sweat.

"Bad dream?" Jayne said, nursing a cup of water, concern on her face. Tom nodded, running his hands through his hair and beard. "Want to talk about it?" She asked. Tom shook his head.

"I need a shower."

A few minutes later, Tom walked downstairs with his hair combed back, his beard washed and his teeth brushed. He looked less of a sasquatch and more of a groomed ape. He walked into the living room with his top off in a pair of loose gym shorts. His wife eyed him from her bed, nearly choking on the bowl of soup she was making her way through.

"Jesus," she said. "Should I be worried? You never walk around like that anymore! I was wondering if all that size under your clothing was just padding!" Tom let out a smile.

"I was hot. I needed to cool down."

"You can turn the fire down," Jayne smiled. "I don't mind." Tom looked out of the window and saw the frost gathering on the glass.

"No," he said. "I'll be fine. You need to keep warm." Tom moved and gave her a kiss on the head, and they shared a look of contentment between them. He gave Jayne the tv remote and checked the time. He had a couple of hours before he had to set out for work. Night shift number two. He was thinking he might actually make it the full week before he knew it. He made a cup of coffee and sat next to Jayne as she settled on a game show where people guess how much money is in boxes.

"I hate this show," she said, putting the remote down. Tom eyed her curiously.

"The hell you put it on for then?" He giggled. Jayne shrugged.

"It's as good as any other crap on the tv these days. Plus, I like it every now and then when they win the big money." The two of them sat in silence for a few minutes watching the contestant cycle through every emotion known to mankind, before walking away with a little over a thousand pounds and them scoffing at the meagre amount.

"They walk in with ten in their pocket and leave with a thousand and they aren't happy," Tom said, sitting back, resting his coffee cup on his oversized gut. He wasn't fat, he was muscular coated in fat. Not like Jerry. Fuck that guy. Tom was prime steak with the fat left on. Jerry was a ball of lard. "Because there's a chance of winning more, people aren't content with what they actually win. Who gives a rat's ass if you could have won ten grand? You have walked out with one hundred times what you went in with." Jayne rolled her eyes. "What?" He said, taking a drink.

"This is why I hate game shows," she said. "So opinionated!" They laughed then. And Tom felt a wave of warmth in her smile.

"So, tell me about your shift?" The two of them spoke about the dullness of the night. He thought about telling her about the footsteps, the book, the dog and even the near-crash he had had on the way home. He thought against it however. He didn't want to worry her.

"Nothing much happened babe. Just sitting on my ass watching screens that didn't move, reading a couple of books I picked up from the store." They continued talking a little longer before Tom clocked the time on the television. He let out a sigh and stood up, stretching himself out. He adjusted Jayne's pillows and duvets and changed her bedpan once more. He did her medication, put the radio on the station she requested, and turned the fire low. He made sure the window was open just a crack but still on the latch to let a little air in, and tucked her sheets in just the way she liked it. He told her he loved her and touched her hands. They were so small inside his. He could feel every knuckle and bone inside that thin skin. He smiled at her and she smiled back. They locked lips, her mouth dry and lips thin, him devouring her in his face bush.

"I love you," he said.

"I love you too," she whispered, just about holding on to staying awake. "I'll see you in the morning." He stepped away, turning the light off, her silhouette illuminated a dark red by the fireplace. He put his key in the lock and pulled the door open, the hit of cold hitting him like the artic wind from that night.

"You better," he whispered, before slipping into the howling night.

10

The Second Night

Tom made another coffee. It was his third one in the last hour. Fuck he was bored. He couldn't even watch movies on his phone because the screen had fucked it in the near-miss the morning before. He had only realised once he had gotten to work, and was running too late to try and go get a replacement for the shift. He had been meaning to write down all his emergency contacts on a piece of paper to keep in his wallet in case something like this happened, something which unfortunately, he had always put off. He was worried at the thought of not being able to contact Jayne if she needed him, but it was only one night, and she had been fine the night before, and she would be fine until the morning. His mind was his own worst enemy, something he had always struggled with. He didn't have anxiety, and was usually never an anxious person, but since the rig, since Brad, the thought of losing someone so close to him, knowing he could do something to prevent it, would be something he couldn't go through ever again.

He wandered around a little, stretched his legs, before returning to the only fun he could have had outside of masturbating at work, reading the book he found inside the cupboard. He had gotten a fair way through it tonight, seeing as it was the only thing he could do to stop himself from either drifting off or start reading a newspaper. Fuck that, he had enough shit going on without reading about why the world was fucked or why global warming was going to kill everyone in the next thirty years.

"And as I found myself observing the blackness around me, I couldn't help but feel the touch of snow on my bare skin. I needed to find something

soon, someone to pull me from this nightmare, for then I could truly dream of warmer days."

Tom put the book down and regretted what he had thought about the book being decent. It was not. There were tonnes of spelling mistakes, most of it was withered and he couldn't understand what was being said, and not to mention the absolute dribble it was filled with that didn't seem to go anywhere. No wonder it didn't have the author's name on it. Nobody would ever want to put their name to having spent hours writing such utter bullshit. He put the book down and checked through the cameras. Everything still. He checked the time. 1 am.

"Still a long way to go," he whispered, rubbing his eyes. He took hold of the torch and exited the SEC RITY room.

The beam from the torch licked the walls and shelves of the abandoned office, the busted clock in the corner stuck at '03:15.' He had read a story about that once, about a man who loses his wife and is haunted by her memory. It didn't end well, so Tom stopped thinking about it. The office gave him the creeps. He imagined the monitors sparking on for a second and going dead again. He imagined seeing the draws fly open and papers spill out onto the ground. He imagined –

Shut up! He told that monkey in his brain to stop banging on the cymbals for ten fucking minutes. His mind was going into overdrive tonight, the worry in his heart bleeding into his thoughts.

He opened the office door into the main warehouse and made the rounds along the walkways and shelving. He saw Gretta, the sorting machine. Its mechanical teeth not looking too friendly, and Tom dreaded to think what was left of that poor bastard's hand once Gretta had had his way with him.

    The office areas were next. He put the keys in the lock and pushed the doors open, giving a cursory glance around the abandoned desks of HR, Payroll and Human Sacrifice. Then he went to the canteen, the backyard which was fenced off and had a few bicycles chained to the walls. Dusting the falling snow from his coat, he went to the back rooms where the elevator led down to the storage area of the unwanted mail. The ride wasn't nice. The elevator was a tiny box with a pull gate you had to manually secure yourself which rattled and shook violently when the ride got moving. All those years of dragging and hauling parcels down had taken their toll. Tom didn't want to think how long he would be trapped alone in the dark should the damn thing stop working. When the elevator made it to its destination, he threw the door open and jumped out like it was going to plummet to the depths of hell.

The storage room was more organised than Tom would have thought: boxes and mail stacked up in order of dates, locations and the amount of time they had been sitting there. Tom could see a few things poking out from behind the withered cardboard: watches, appliances, skates, shoes. All sorts of things. He made a mental note to jot this down when he got back to his desk. He's sure Jayne would love to see what she could find down here. He finished his rounds in the darkness, shitting himself on one occasion when a rat as big as a small dog ran from under the shelving, darting past him until the little furry bastard disappeared under a racking filled with stacks of toilet paper. He moved back to the elevator, then thinking better of it, decided to take the stairs. He didn't want to risk pushing the elevator too far. Plus he needed to pee, the cups of coffee coming back to say hello.

The stairs were freshly cleaned and the smell of bleach permeated the air. The cleaners must finish right before he starts. About halfway up those spiralling steps, he heard something which made his ball sack tighten to a tight set of plums. Footsteps coming up behind him.

Like his arse hole was rimmed with chilli flakes, he bolted up those damn stairs three at a time, the burning in his legs screaming for him to stop until he reached the top doors, pushing them open and stood away from the doors, waiting for whatever cocksucker was coming up behind him to show themselves where Tom would meet them with a face full of *fuck you!* Nothing came however, and as the minutes passed he began to doubt he had heard anything at all. The building was big, empty, and his footsteps would have made one hell of a racket. Easy enough to think that his own footsteps could be carried further, bouncing back into his ears and duplicated through some magic of physics he didn't understand. He turned his back on those doors, expecting some fiend from hell to burst through, dragging him down the stairs back to the basement, kicking and screaming. But he shook the thoughts away. He even laughed a little to himself, continuing his rounds, not wanting to look back to those doors in case it was stood there. He could feel it, his old friend again. It building up inside his stomach, soaking into his veins and nestling to the back of his head, and for a very real moment he felt something unmistakable.

Fear.

11
Later

Tom wasn't one for worrying about things that go bump in the night. When you've spent as much time alone in the dark as he had, the night became your friend. When the salt air mixes with the whisky in your blood, the world seems that little brighter. But tonight he was sober, as he had been for many months now. Eleven months, eleven days and six hours. Not like he was counting. So maybe that's why he was starting to feel a little on edge? He felt his hands beginning to tremble as he held the torch and his brow start to sweat despite the cool air. He stopped and held his hand up in the dim light. He hadn't had the shakes since he had put the bottle down for good. Why was it happening to him now? He forced the thought of downing a few cold ones to the bottom of his mind, stomped on it a few times then threw it in the incinerator. He wasn't going to think about booze, no matter how much he felt the thirst all the fucking time. Tom got back to the SEC RITY room and grabbed the notepad.

Tuesday 00:12

I freaked myself out before babe. I was down in the basement doing the rounds and I didn't trust the elevator. I used the stairs. The smell of bleach was way too much for me to handle, I think it made my head go a little funny because I heard those footsteps again, like I heard outside on the first night. I think this place is driving me crazy, and I've only been here for two nights. Not to mention, *and I don't want to admit this, but I have been thinking a lot about the rig and what happened, and I feel I might relapse.*

He stared at those words under the dull light of the grey monitors. *I think I might relapse.* The thought of him going home to his wife who is having her body radiated so much he was surprised she didn't glow in the dark, and tell her he wanted to drink again because he had a bad time at sea made him feel sick. He tore out the page and threw it in the trash. He got the pen again –

I keep thinking of you while I'm here. Tonight has been tough knowing I can't call you. But I know you're okay.

I haven't seen anything on the monitors yet. Nothing but empty space. The snow is falling a lot though. Good job I brought a shovel with me for the morning.

Tom put the pen down and watched the monitors, giving them a quick flick through. All was quiet initially, but as he looked over the parking lot camera, he saw it. The dog was back, its head sniffing around the back of Tom's pickup that was slowly looking like an Igloo. Tom eyed the beast. It must be freezing, but he remembered what Jerry had said about the other guy feeding the animals that came wandering around the grounds. Tom touched the pages of his journal and he suddenly felt the creeping urge to write a little more. To revive that screwed up page, its words needing to be told. He fought internally, and after a minute, he pulled open a new page.

I can't help keep thinking about him. About Brad and what happened. I know it wasn't my fault. But that doesn't seem to comfort me much.

Tom put the pen back down. He didn't feel like writing anymore.

12

Later

He sat and watched the dog for a few minutes. It had been circling the back of Tom's truck, sniffing at the back door and then licking the bottom of his wheel. Maybe he had ran over a rabbit or something on the way in? Or maybe he had dropped a snack when he grabbed his bag earlier. The poor thing must have been freezing. The image wasn't crystal clear, and Tom could still see the dog's bones pushing through its fur. It was curled up under the bottom of the truck now, hardly visible to the camera.

Tom felt his heart begin to swell, like someone had dropped a hot coal in a frozen pond. The warmth spreading to his chest and out to his fingertips. He couldn't bring the dog inside, but he had more than enough snacks to see him through the next few hours. It was a little past midnight, and the cleaner would be coming in around six, before the day staff took over at seven. He didn't have long left before he could go home back to his wife. And he wouldn't feel right if he spent the next six or seven hours watching the poor animal freeze under his car without anything to eat.

Tom rummaged through his rucksack and found a pack of mini sausages. The pack was the kind you normally buy if you were having a small buffet or hell, going away for the weekend in a camper. He let his mind drift back to the year him and Jayne had met. She was studying at university, some degree he couldn't possibly begin to understand, while he was working as a mechanic at the local car garage. He booked the weekend off work, or so Tom told her. Really he just phoned in sick and played hooky for a few shifts. They travelled to Galloway National Park in Scotland and lay under the sun in the evening warmth. They spoke of the star signs, the meaning of life, and the vastness of the black that loomed above them, a blanket of space scattered with millions of tiny diamonds, all so far away they could be long dead. Like an echo of what once was, an echo of something no longer around but you can still feel its presence if you listen close enough.

  He did now as he did then, always packing way too much to eat. So as Tom eyed the pack of sausages mixed in with an assortment of other goodies: Oreos, cookies, crisps, dried meats and sandwiches. He felt much better about giving some to the dog. It wasn't having the Oreos though. They were his. The dog could have the apple too if it really wanted, but he didn't think even the animal was *that* desperate just yet.

  He grabbed the sausages and went for the exit, but turned back, checked over the rest of the monitors to make sure the shadows hadn't grown teeth. He mentally checked himself, telling him that he was fine. It was all in his head. The dead weren't lurking in anywhere other than his mind. And still, as he thought this, he took the baseball bat out of his bag anyway.

  It took around eight minutes to walk from the SEC RITY room to the front entrance of the building, and in that time Tom had managed to scare the shit out of himself at least twice. The first was immediately after he exited the office and saw his reflection in the surrounding office window. His face looked to be aged and ragged, and his beard, albeit already showing signs of grey, was completely whitewashed. He looked in his sixties, and his thick jacket looked ashen and weathered. His skin looked grey and his face withered, his eyes sunken. Tom squoze his eyes tight and looked again to find him still looking as ugly as ever.

  The second time was he thought he had forgotten his pass for the front door, and then the thought crept into his mind of not being able to get back in should the doors close behind him. He found the pass around his neck, and swiftly told the intruding thoughts to *fuck off*.

  The dog was still outside by the time Tom got to the main doors. The night was silent and the car park still. The snow had stopped falling and the sky above was clear. A good sign. It would still be as cold as dick when Tom left in a few hours, but at least he wasn't snowed in, which meant the dog should be okay too. He pressed the green button to exit the foyer and the hit of cold air made his boys shrivel up in his pants.

Tom whistled to the dog and it poked its head from under the truck. He dropped the pack of sausages down on the ground near the kerb of the car park and stepped back inside the building. The dog, seeing him now gone and food left there for the taking, emerged from under the truck and stalked cautiously to the meal. Tom crouched in the dark, staying still. The dog was actually pretty damn big despite it being withered. It was a Doberman: Its eyes a light brown, almost a dull green. Its fur was sleek and its ears pointed. Paws made firm indents in the snow and its snout pushed hot air into the surrounding cold. Tom felt that little better as the animal wolfed up the meal and retreated back into the car park and vanished into the tree line, the string of sausages hanging from its mouth. He stood, the cold seeping into his joints, and went back to the SEC RITY room, but not before taking a leak in the solitary toilet everyone was raving about.

13
Dawn

Tom once again found himself reading the book which he said he hated. He was a fair few pages in and frankly, was only reading it until the boss could come and tell him he could leave for the day. The main character, whose identity was still unknown, was lost in the trees and was looking for somewhere to sleep. The night was unrelenting, and from what Tom could fathom, there was something following him through the trees –

"I try to ignore the feeling that I am being followed, but it keeps returning to my mind over and over, like a mosquito you swat away but can't quite get rid of. It keeps coming back, and when I turn to check I am safe, I see no monsters behind me and the darkness does not grow teeth. No eyes of red glare at me, and the trees do not clutch at me with their finger like branches that bow overhead. But yet as I trudge through this never-ending night, the stars over me shining, and the moon low, swollen and red, I feel that there is something that wishes to do me harm. Be that from the outside world, or the monster within my own mind."

"Tom!" The loud voice bolstered Tom out of his seat. Jerry stood there, his clothes layered with snowflakes. "Jesus I was shouting you for about a minute!" His face was red and his nostrils flared. "The second time now I find you staring at a book and not at the monitors? What the hell is wrong with you?"

"What time is it?" Tom said, confused about why Jerry was here so early in the morning. "You're early aren't you?" Jerry's temper seemed to surge greater.

"The fuck? You don't know what time it is? It's fucking seven-thirty Tom! You fall asleep or something?"

"Seven-thirty?" Tom repeated with horror, his mind trying to find where his time had gone. He had only just fed the dog, came in and sat down and was watching the monitors. Now he found himself missing three hours, face in a book he didn't care for, and the boss shouting at him asking to account for why the fuck he wasn't paying attention. "I'm sorry," Tom said, packing up his things. He took a drink of his coffee he had just made to find it stone cold. So cold in fact, the lip of the cup had gathered frost.

"It's freezing in here; did you not put the heater on?" Jerry said, rubbing his hands together.

"Yeah, I…" Tom whispered to himself. Did he? It was a few below freezing last night. He was so stiff. Where had the time gone?

"Whatever," Jerry said dismissively. "Get home and tonight, I want you here that little earlier. I've got a few things to shoot out and do before you start your shift and we can't leave the place unmanned. I need you here for five, not seven. That okay?" He said, raising an eyebrow.

"Absolutely," Tom said, packing the last bits of his things up, putting the book back into the drawer. "I'll be here."

The ride back home was treacherous at best. The road had really begun to freeze up, but at least Tom didn't have a damn mobile phone to distract him this time. He still saw some cars in the snow, crawling morning traffic playing Candy Crush or some other shite on their devices behind the wheel, often needing to break at the last moment because they hadn't realised that the car in front had stopped moving a few seconds ago. Tom even leant out the window and blasted his horn at one driver in front of him who was reading something on an iPad whilst holding a cigarette in one hand and a cup of coffee in the other. He didn't give a fuck if he was driving a Tesla. It wasn't the point. It was the principle of the damn thing.

He arrived home a little before nine. The house was again all in darkness and as he went through the door, he noticed that the house was stone cold. Fear crept along Tom's flesh. He left the front door ajar, stepping in with snow-covered boots.

"Jayne?" He said, trying to hide the trembling in his voice. He stepped into the living room, turning the corner of the door. His breath caught in his throat. He ran to her, picking her up from the floor, her half-naked body covered in soiled blankets and sheets from the tipped bedpan. Her body cold to touch. He remembered screaming, running out into the street, begging a passer-by for a phone to use. He raced inside, touching her cold face, her lips turned a light shade of blue and screaming to the ambulance on the phone that she wasn't breathing.

14
Tie Those Boots

The paramedics came bursting through the door a few minutes after he had called them. He told them the address, and that his wife wasn't breathing. He wasn't completely sure, his mind a blur, not wanting to look into his wife's vacant eyes as they stared at the grey ceiling above. He shouted her name, stricken with worry, like all his muscles in his body were tightening at once, unable to release any tension.

They pulled him from her, taking over. Three of them converged onto Jayne, jamming IV drips into her arms whilst the other attached an oxygen mask and pumped a plastic balloon, forcing air into her lungs. They attached wires and mechanisms that beeped and buzzed, her vitals showing on a small machine that they carried with them. The paramedics exchanged a grave look, and then without a second's hesitation, began CPR. Tom heard the cracking and splintering of his wife's ribs, a sound that shattered though any remaining resolve or hope that she would be okay, that she was just sleeping or in some kind of coma. They pressed over and over and then pulled her onto a gurney, one paramedic at all times keeping the sickening rhythm on her chest, her body moving out like a dead fish being slapped with a mallet before being served to hungry fishermen.

They raced outside, pushing the gurney between them, Tom pacing close behind. In the back of the ambulance, the harsh light pierced Tom's night time eyes, his body running on fumes and redlining with fear and adrenaline. The technician dove into the driver's seat and the paramedics put a seatbelt around the gurney so Jayne wouldn't go anywhere, oxygen being forced into her lungs that were being massaged by a very red-faced first responder, him cursing at the unbreathing body in front of him.

They spoke so fast between themselves, all kinds of measurements being thrown out and being scribbled down on green paper: heart rate, blood pressure, carbon dioxide levels, toxicity of the blood, amongst other things. Tom stood helpless, like he was watching his wife be ravaged by wolves and he could do nothing but watch and hope they didn't take her too far over the edge.

The ambulance fired into life and the technician sped away, blaring the sirens as fast as she could without colliding with parked cars and standing traffic. The sirens filled the air as they hurtled in that tiny box which buzzed and blared, rocking and knocking them off their feet when the driver had to take evasive action.

"Do you know CPR?" The red-faced paramedic shouted breathlessly. Tom looked around; she was talking to him. This was his turn now, to drive his boulder hands into his Jayne's withered bag of bones wrapped in thin flesh. Her eyes still open, lips turning paler. He shook his head, feeling so small in a big world. The paramedic gave him a crash course, and on the count of three, Tom drove those sasquatch hands into his wife's sternum and began to press one third into her body at a rate of two compressions a second. He pushed and felt the crack of the ribs under his hands. He pulled back, the feeling cutting through him, knocking him sick. "Keep going!" The breathless paramedic said, wiping his face on his rubber gloves. "It's going to hurt her, but she'll just be sore. Better that than…" Tom didn't want to hear the next word. He dove on her once more, going hell for leather. His wife of thirty years, her life was in his hands, quite literally. He felt like he could cup her heart and massage it back to health. She had helped him through his addiction, got him away from crime, even when he was a wreck coming back from the rig. Now it was his turn to save *her*. He pressed down on that motherfucker like his own life depended on it. If she didn't pull through, then he wouldn't have a life left, and the bottle would soon be calling his name once more.

The ambulance flew through the grey streets, maneuvering through streams of solid brake lights and pedestrians trying to wade through the thickening snow. After what seemed like a lifetime, Tom was pulled away as more doctors and nurses from the ER burst through the back doors of the ambulance and pulled him away, taking over from him. He hadn't noticed they were at the ambulance bay at the hospital. A ride into hell that never seemed to end. Tom moved back, rushing after the squeaking trolley and the worried faces of the nurses that attached more probes, paramedics firing jargon faster than Tom could understand the sounds coming out their mouths to the doctors that hastily wrote it all down on their clip boards. They asked Tom some details about his wife: name, date of birth, address, blood type, medical history, and next of Kin. Tom tried all he could but he was still walking, his thoughts running faster than a bunch of squirrels that had been set alight. They pushed through the ER reception doors and Tom saw the myriad of terrified and worried eyes that fell onto him, and he had never felt more out of depth in his life. Being stranded at sea was nothing compared to this, he was sweating, his clothes sticking to him, his adrenaline spiking and pupils dilating. He was breathless, catching himself on the reception desk, steadied by two security guards dressed in black body armour. They got him a chair, but he tried to fight them, screaming her name as she disappeared with doctors and nurses through a set of double doors, hearing them shout to do another shock, that she was flat lining.

15
The Third Night

Tom stared at the greyscale computer monitor with as much enthusiasm as a dog being told to give its favourite toy back. Nothing was moving, and the snow had fallen quickly since he had arrived at Welch Mill. The car park had been cleared by the shift before him, shovelling the white stuff in heaps and piling them on the side of the car park in huge mounds. Grit laid on the tarmac and the exiting cars scarring the remaining snow in thick black lines. They had since been frosted over, until they were now completely buried once more. Tom's truck sitting alone near the front of the building, shivering its mechanical arse off, coated in thick white. Tom thought of Jayne.

"You need to go back in tonight," she had said once she had woken up. She was a mess; her chest was bandaged and she had more wires and tubes poking out of her than a fuse box after a rat had gotten to it. "You need to go and take care of yourself. I am in the best place possible here. Sitting here will only make you worry." Tom sat by her bedside, listening to the various beeping and buzzing going off from the machines she was hooked up too. He stared at the floor, looking back at his reflection in the linoleum, the smell of citrus and bleach assaulting his nostrils.

"I should have been home," he whispered, trying not to crack. "I should have been at home with you last night. I could have done something; I could have helped you." He felt her fingers run through his long hair.

"Now you stop thinking like that Sash," she said. "You know that you couldn't have known what was going to happen, and that you did all you could. I am glad you got home when you did. The paramedics said that you saved my life."

"I should have been home," Tom said again bitterly. "I would have helped more. How do I know something like that isn't going to happen again?" He looked at her, his eyes bloodshot.

"The doctors have given me some extra medication to take for my heart. It's the cancer... it spread to my lungs and put pressure on the heart which stopped it beating for a short while." She sounded like she was talking about the latest upset in a reality TV show.

"How can you be so fucking calm Jayne?" He seethed, pressing his hands into the thin blanket. "You could have died. The damn doctors didn't spot the tumour was growing, didn't spot that your heart was under strain. This is their fault." He was caving into himself now, his stern exterior crumbling, the stone statue withered by the storm that just wouldn't stop beating it until it eroded and cracked. She touched his hands, leaning into him.

"You need to stop being so hard on yourself. You couldn't have known. No one could have! It happened, and I am fine."

"I'm going to quit the security job," he said, shaking his head. "I'm going to declare that I'm your full-time carer. You need the help now more than ever." Jayne let out a sigh.

"We both know that that wouldn't be good," she said. "You need to keep busy. You need to be out of the house. You need something to keep you occupied." Tom let the words sink in. She was right. As much as he didn't want to admit it, she was right, as she always was. She was always the one that had the clearer, more rational head. *Sash smash*, as she would often say when Tom would think the best way to handle a situation was to throw might rather than reason at it. This was one of those occasions and given by the bandages around his wife's ribs, Sash had smashed enough today.

An hour later, he managed to get a little sleep in the rigid uncomfortable waiting chair next to her bed whilst she got some rest herself. She would be in the hospital for a few days at most, then brought back home. Tom had agreed to stay working only if his wife had more care when he wasn't there, to which the home care company happily agreed, for an increased fee of course. Tom returned home after that, driving carefully on the roads that were growing more treacherous by the hour.

In his home he turned the light on, and the sight of the overturned bed and spilled bedpan made him weak at the knees. He cried then, allowed himself to breathe and let it out. He had nearly lost her. The realisation rampaging in his mind. He had nearly lost the woman he has woken up too every day for the last thirty years, other than his years at the rig. He got to work on cleaning the carpet and the sheets. Then, he eyed the large stack of half opened debt letters on his side table and realised Jayne was completely right. They had lived in the same house for last twenty years. They had always wanted children, but he had issues with his swimmers, and the IVF was too expensive, so they settled on a dog instead. Jasper, a little Yorkshire terrier. He had died a few years back after a long and happy life. Tom went to go work on the rigs shortly after that. When he got back, the doctor told him that the lump on his wife's breast wasn't just a cyst, and they had to remortgage the house to pay for the treatment. Eyeing those letters that hissed like a pile of rattlesnakes, he knew that Jayne was right. Those wolves were howling at his door and he needed to keep them at bay.

Tom sat back in his chair, sleep wanting to find him. He checked the clock. It was only 9 PM. He had a long shift ahead of him and needed to keep himself busy. Should the boss Jerry come back unannounced and find him sleeping on the job, it was bye bye salary, bye bye extra care for Jayne, and hello repossession letters.

He got to his feet, stretched himself out and gave the monitors one last flick through and seeing nothing but greyscale, left the SEC RITY room. He walked through the main office and into the warehouse. The sound of the wind rattled the large doors which let the wagons come through and the building creaked and ached with him. Tom shone his torch on the racking. He eyed frost appearing on the shelving, and knew that it was only going to get worse. Then, he spotted a small pool of icy water on the floor. He found a mop and wiped that sucker dry, putting out a wet floor sign, before the damn thing froze and became an ice rink.

Moving through the rest of the building, he found a small electric heater in the CEO's office and hauled it back to the SEC RITY room where he hooked it up, relaxing with a cup of hot coffee. Now, he had to fight off boredom. His phone was still busted, and he sat with the office phone next to him, hooked up to the wall. He had given the hospital his work's landline, another condition of him returning to work this evening, against all reservations. He hadn't even thought to bring any snacks or real food other than a small bag of spiced sausages he had bought at the deli counter of the gas station he had fuelled up in on the way to work. He tucked into one of the tiny delightful bastards. His stomach rumbled, yearning for fulfilment. He hadn't eaten in nearly 48 hours, and he was running on fumes. The spiced meat filled his mouth and he inhaled the morsel, hunger ravaging his body as he tucked into them famished, washing them down with a hot cup of coffee. He felt good, his mood getting better with the heat and the food. He felt a feeling of calm come over him. He put the rest of the pack back into his bag.

I could kill for a drink, he thought. *A nice little scotch with a little ice. 12 years aged. Beer or two to chase it down.* He shook his head, noticing that again, his hands were trembling. He held them steady. Why was he thinking again about the drink? Was it the stress? The job? The long hours alone or more likely, the fact his wife is dying? He remembered what his sponsor at the AA meetings had told him: *'You gotta keep busy. The bottle is the vulture on your shoulder. If you give it enough attention, it will get heavier until you can't ignore it.*

Easy for him to say, Tom thought. Try keeping away when you have your wife in hospital, in fuck tonnes of debt and you haven't slept properly in months. He didn't mean to, but without realising, he had opened up the authorless book from the drawer of his desk, and was falling into the pages before he realised.

'I move quickly, my assailant soon behind me. I come to a clearing, my friend nowhere to be found, by this creature that follows me in this black, a friend they are not. He stands tall, withered and thin, a long grey beard and grey jellied eyes of blind man.'

'"Back beast!" I call, standing, facing my foe, hiding the fear in my voice. "I vanquish you to the hell you came! God has my side, and his light will force you back into the black which you spawned from!" I call and pray to my Lord, yet the creature does not retreat into the black. Its shoulders click and its thin ribs push through withered skin. Its face that of a man, an elderly man, its nose curved to its top lip, pointed and sharp. Its teeth bared, lines of yellow nubs pushing through blackened lips. Its fingers long, bony, nails sharp. It eyes me, then in my tongue, utters to me –'

'"Death is an echo. I may be vanquished by your false God, but I will remain until my debt is repaid." I turn to run, but the creature is there again in front of me. The blood moon above swelling once more, as the trees grow vines that strike me, wrapping around my legs and wrists.'

Tom turned the page. The last part of the story was missing. "What fucking dip shit tears out the back of a book?" He cursed, feeling the calmness that had befallen him melt like the falling snow. Tom opened the cupboard and tossed the book into the top drawer. He drove his hand into his duffel bag and pulled out his journal.

Wednesday. Night shift number three.

The last place on earth where I want to be is here. My wife is in the hospital and I am here sitting on my ass away from her through the night time hours, alone with my thoughts and a book that has no ending. Someone tore the pages out. Sadists.

The doctors said she would be fine, and I guess I have to give a little faith to them. They do wear lab coats and have thousands of pounds of student loan debt to justify their expert opinion after all. But I don't want to be here. I cleaned the house before I left, so that when I can go to the hospital and get her, I don't have as much to do. Fuck I'm tired. I haven't slept much at all since starting this job, never mind the last day. That was rough. Seeing her like that.

Anyway, I need the money, and what a shit state of affairs it is when a husband must be away from his wife to pay for the care she needs? She said that it does me good, keeping away, keeping my mind occupied, less I decide to drink again. And I guess she is right. But my god do I miss it.

Sorry, I thought I heard something. Why am I apologising to you? Sounded like something fell over in the other room. Just checked the monitors and nothing was there. Must be the wind or a rat or something. Ugh. I want to get this night over with, and it's still early yet. No food, no phone. It's going to be a long one... After I get my first pay cheque, I am out of this place. Jayne needs me.

He went to write more, but he caught something move on the monitors out the corner of his eye. The greyscale flickering, something emerging from the tree line. The dog. It was back.

16
Tread Lightly Kids

"Jesus," Tom spat with a shaky jaw. He hadn't noticed on the camera or through the thick glass of the automatic doors, but the sky had really clouded over. The thick spiralling blackness above him was giving way to a behemoth of snow, like a giant head of hair having a good scratch, getting the nails right in there and the flakes of skin peppering the world below. The snow was gathering around Tom's boots, and he knew that it would be there to stay. He wondered if he had brought some de-icer and a shovel, but in a warehouse this large he was sure they would have something to help him out. A hammer and chisel, a flamethrower, sulphuric acid. He'd find something.

The dog was curled up underneath the bed of the pickup truck. Tom crunched the ground as he moved closer, hearing the electronic doors close behind him. At the back of the passenger side rear wheel, Tom eyed a clump of fur and a bloodstain frozen to the rubber mangled into the trim. He must have caught a rabbit on the way in, the smell of a free meal finding the starving pooches' nostrils.

Tom pulled a couple of sausages he had saved from his pocket. They weren't much, but he couldn't sit by and watch the dog starve to death. Not in weather like this. The wind bit his fingers something nasty, icy teeth cutting into his skin and gnawing on the bone. He held out the meat to the shivering beast which perked its head up and bared its teeth.

Tom placed another down by his feet and took a step back. The Doberman, its fur short, ears pointed and legs long, crept from under the truck and skulked forward, checking the coast was clear, before devouring the sausage once more.

Finally, Tom thought to be ballsy. If he was freezing his ass off outside and treating this runaway to some of the finest processed food money can buy from the reduced section at the local garage, God damn it he was gonna pet the damn thing even if it meant losing a finger. Figuratively speaking of course. Tom took another sausage, took a small bite and held it out in his hand. The Doberman was hesitant, those ears once more flattening, that tail tucking between thin quaking legs.

"It's okay," Tom said softly. "Come on." He wiggled the weaner in his fingers. The Doberman reared closer and with the swiftness of a spoilt child at a birthday party, snatched the meat quickly, its teeth gracing the end of Tom's fingers making him wince. It trotted back a couple of paces and ate the meat, not taking its eyes off the man with the big black coat and the baseball bat poking out the top of it. "Little shit," Tom joked to himself putting his bloodied fingers in his mouth. "Probably need a tetanus."

Tom turned and walked towards the front doors. The single street light illuminating him and the ever-gathering snow by his feet. Tom turned and saw the dog had gone, once again either hiding under his truck or had disappeared into the surrounding wood. He smiled to himself, saying farewell to his new nighttime buddy. He pulled out the pass from around his neck, touching the final sausage he had saved for himself in his jacket pocket.

He touched the black box which went from solid red to blinking green, making the glass doors open with a low whoosh. He went to step in when he heard the panting. He turned to see the dog once more, this time leaping for his hand, taking the meat from him. Tom recoiled, falling backwards onto the ground, snow hitting his face and the sting of concrete caressing his cheek. Dazed, he looked about the falling white on black, and saw the doors of the main entrance closing. He sat up, scrambling to wedge them open with his bat, but its head missed the last opening of the doors.

Tom eyed the Doberman through the glass, it sitting, panting. Its long tongue falling from those hungry snapping jaws. It shook the melting snow from itself, then disappeared into the black hallways, Tom's security pass attached to its paw, dragging him with it, his 2 x 5 picture smiling away at the world. He touched the frosting glass of the doors.

"Fuck."

17
Watch Your Step

Tom sat up and brushed the gathering snow from his beard, holding the side of his head where he had made out with the concrete and gotten a bad hickey as a result. "The fuck am I going to do now?" He cursed to himself, frustrated with his stupidity more than anything else. He stood and moved to the black glass, thinking somehow they would open for him, but they didn't budge. Tom thought about smashing the glass open, but that was one way to get fired, and a sure way to lose what little money he would get from his first paycheque. *Sash Smash* he thought to himself. He snarled again "Fuck!"

The building was huge, and he could feel the might of the clouds falling onto him. He was hungry, and the real fear of freezing to death crept into his mind. It was far below zero degrees, and he had left his keys inside the office so he couldn't sit tight in his truck for the night.

Jayne entered his mind. Him lying in the corner trying to keep warm until the morning staff arrived. The cold hooking into his bones. The police telling Jayne he was found stiff, his face fixed in a permanent scream of her name. Tom pressed his hands to his temples and told the thoughts and images to disappear before he made them with his bat. *Think Tom,* he pressed himself. *There must be another way in.* Tom moved to the edge of the building and was met with a large wire fence where a security camera sat iced over, bleeping its red light on its big black eye. He studied the area but nothing jumped out at him. He couldn't climb something that large, not with how cold he was. Even if he managed to get to the top of the wire mesh fence with his fingers intact, there was still the problem of the huge loops of razor wire to contend with. He had seen what they can do to a man if they hook just the right part. Again he shook the memories from his mind.

"Fuck!" He hissed into the wind. He scrunched his face up tight, looking at the other security camera blinking at him. Tom saw a break in the razor wire, about half a foot long. At the base of the wall, there was a pile of empty storage boxes and a tonne of cigarette butts. Tom pressed the boxes with his bat and they were frozen solid, coated in a thick layer of snow. He picked up a couple, shaking the snow from them and bundled them under his arm, remembering his burglary days in his twenties.

The wind broke the still silence as its icy tongue licked his numbing face. He gripped hold of the wire mesh with his bare hands and the cold metal sliced through his flesh, sending a harsh burn through his fingertips. He felt the blood draining from his white knuckles as he took a handful of the wiring and hauled his frozen legs up from the ground. Another handful and the snow pelted his face a little more. The fence rattled under his weight like someone jingling a huge rung of old keys, the shaking fence dancing in the night, showering snow on the ground below. A little higher he went, and he could feel his fingers beginning to give way. He gritted his teeth, forcing the frozen digits to take another handful, before he was top side, the glint of the razor wire staring him in the face like a game of chicken with a great white shark, daring him to try his luck.

He took the cardboard and placed it in the gap of the wiring and placed it as flat as he could. Then, with one final yearning effort, he pulled himself onto the cardboard and flopped over the other side like a beached killer whale snagging a sleeping seal.

"Hey!" The voice slammed into Tom's ears like a dog singing a nursery rhyme. Tom missed the mesh on the other side and fell to the ground. He tumbled, grabbing out at anything but only finding air. He collided with the frozen ground, hard. He lay there for a moment, the wind knocked out of him, covered in snow and cardboard. A flashlight illuminated his face from the other side of the fence.

"What are you doing here? You're not allowed here! I'm calling the police!" Tom hauled his ass up to his feet and eyed the man's darkened face. He was wearing similar clothing to him: dark jacket with blue jeans. His face was obscured by the blinding light being shone in Tom's eyes.

"I fucking work here man!" Tom bellowed through the wind. "A damn dog took my pass so I had to find another way in!"

"Bullshit!" The torch wielding man said. "I saw you from across the way, scoping the place out! The fuck you got a baseball bat for if you work security? You're tryna rob the place?" With that, the torch man took out his phone and turned away from Tom. He put it to his ear and Tom heard him on the phone to the police.

"Yeah call the cops, I'm gonna get back to my warm desk. Let me know when they turn up." Tom turned on his heel and continued on, "now fuck off." The back courtyard had tonnes of empty boxes stacked up against steel railings with more spikes you can shake a stick at, two open trailers left by HGV's, and giant dumpsters. Tom eyed windows lining the upper floor of the place, too high to reach, and he didn't feel like risking a climb again, his back throbbing like a snare drum on raw nerves. The torch man's voice yammering away in the background, carried away by the wind. He would have a story to tell the police when they got here. Those blue lights flickering on the horizon in the night. *Boom boom.*

A thought struck him. He knew his wife's number by heart, and the guy with the torch had a phone. Maybe he could let him use it? Doubtful, but this was all a misunderstanding. He was in the security uniform of the place after all and his car was in the damn parking lot. He would be able to talk his way through it. Where had the guy come from anyway? There wasn't another building around here for at least five miles.

Tom turned to shout the guy, but he saw no torch. He walked to the fence wiring again and got a good view of the parking lot. The guy was nowhere to be seen.

"Hey!" Tom called into the night. He moved to the wiring, pressing his face against the frozen metal, trying to find where the spectre had vanished too. Then he felt it. The pain in his leg. He looked up to the top of the fence. The cardboard had gone, and there was no hole in the wiring. Wet heat gathered around his quad. He looked down at the razor wire buried in his upper thigh, and the pool of crimson soaking onto the white blanket under his quivering feet.

18
Razor Wire Wet Kiss

The next few minutes of Tom Mackenzie's life were a runaway freight train of holy fuck. Tom began to spiral, his heartbeat redlining. He gripped the razor wire with his bare hands and tore them to pieces trying to pull them out. He screamed more than a sailor with a bad hangover and then some. Stumbling, limping, him haemorrhaging into the abyssal white that surrounded him. His head spun, the ground meeting his back, snow pelting his face. Hot air spilling from his mouth and the darkening patch around his jeans.

Digging his bloodied numb fingers into the ground, he crawled and dragged his ass to the back door of the warehouse which was sealed tight. With all his strength, he took out his bat and flogged the glass of the window. A bullseye appeared, so he hit it again and again until the glass gave way. He pushed the head of the bat through the hole and pushed the glass out of the way which shattered loudly on the concrete floor on the other side.

The alarm was deafening, wailing and bright flashing red lights bounced around his vision, casting deep red glows in the inside floor and shelving. He slammed his hand through the gap and fumbled numbly for the deadbolt. He found it and pulled as hard as he could. His teeth bared, leg drenching his junk in red hot, he forced the door free which came away reluctantly, covered in frost and ice.

He fell through the gap and splayed in the dark and glowing red. He clambered to his feet, leaving the mouth of the building wide open, allowing the ravenous winter blizzard to follow him through the racks of shelving. He got to the solitary bathroom at the back of the warehouse and pulled free the door. He hit the light and the porcelain white walls with stains from God knows what orifice greeted him like a dirty protest in a prison cell. Tom collapsed onto the freezing cold vinyl and tore open his jeans a little farther. He grabbed a small hand towel and wrapped it around his hands, then for good measure, put the handle of his bat in his mouth. He screamed and agonised behind the metal handle, digging his teeth deep into its leather grip as he took hold of the wire and forced it out, it gliding across his bone and tearing into his skin, hooking muscle and fat, flesh and fabric. The wire came loose finally, and Tom let out a breath of air, but he wasn't out the woods yet. He grabbed a bottle of disinfectant from the side of the ruined toilet bowl, unscrewed it, and poured it onto the fleshy wound.

If the razor wire hurt like a bitch, then the burn of the disinfectant was the bitch's ugly fuck of an uncle. Red hot flames poured onto his skin and danced around his thigh, sending shocks of fire through his body as he rattled against the wall, screaming to whatever would listen to go fuck itself. Lastly, he grabbed a handful of paper towels and stuffed them into the wound, and then wrapped the hand towel over it as an improvised bandage. He tried to hold on a moment before passing out.

19
The Phantom

The cold touch of a snout on his face woke him up. Tom opened his eyes quickly and recoiled at the sight of a hungry mutt licking his face and at the dried blood on his fingers.

"Fuck off!" Tom screamed at the Doberman, before it trotted away into the night. Tom put his hands to his face. His fingers were numb and blue, and then he felt the shivers start to take hold of him. He climbed to his feet, fighting for every inch of strength and to try and stop his legs giving way, using the bat to prop himself up, less he fumble and his head kiss the porcelain sink. Goodnight round two. Tom put the weight on his good leg. The bandage seemed to have stopped the bleeding, but he didn't want to chance it.

The back door was wide open, but the alarm had stopped. It must have been from a timer or something. He was surprised that it was the dog that woke him up and not the cops. Surely they would have been here by now? Or maybe an ambulance? How long had he been unconscious for? It was still dark out, and the snow seemed to have stopped. It had formed a nice rug of ice on the warehouse floor. Tom made a mental note to leave a wet floor sign at the back door before he went home.

Where was the hole in the fence? The thought hit him like an uninvited guest at a family party. He didn't have the strength to go check for himself, not right now anyway. Maybe he could check on the security cameras? There was one right next to the fence so it should capture the wall. But it *had* been there, otherwise he wouldn't have tried to climb back over. Had he mistaken the gap for something else? And who was the guy outside calling the cops? Nothing made sense at the moment. But regardless, he hadn't bled out, and he was out of the blizzard, so he thanked the heavens for small mercies, no matter how trivial they seemed in the moment.

Tom had never sworn more furiously, more loudly and damn it, more creatively than he did on that long painful walk back to the SEC RITY room. On a better day, he might have been impressed with the amount of different way you could curse all things under the sky, but this didn't seem like the right time for a pat on the back. Tom got into the room and closed the door behind him. By some miracle, his duffel bag was still there and he could still find the tiny amount of nibbles and snacks he had that hadn't been raided by the stray dog roaming the warehouse. He checked the time on the monitors. Only just gone three in the morning. He still had a few hours left before the morning shift came in. "Yeah fucking right," he cursed at the thought of staying another minute in this shit forsaken place. He needed to get out of here and fast. But first, he had a call to make.

He picked up the landline in the SEC RITY room and dialled the hospital ward Jayne was on. The phone began to ring, and in that moment he felt like the silence between the bleeps would eat him alive. Stretching tones of anxiety making his nerve endings like tort violin strings being caressed with a blunt razor blade. The call rang out until an automated message met his numb ears –

"Welcome to Nightingale Hospital. We're sorry, but –" Tom slammed the phone back to the receiver, rubbing his hands on his face. "Fuck," he strained, his mouth arid. Tom sat his ass in the spinning desk chair. He noticed it then. His notebook had been left out, a fresh page staring at him. There, written in scratchy writing read the word –

'*Home.*'

Tom stared at the offending word in the dull light of the monitor. Had he written that? No, he hadn't. He would remember. But then again, he hadn't slept properly in nearly three days. The stress, the anxiety, the loneliness. The *fear*. He turned the pages of the journal and horror ripped through him. Every page. Every fucking page.

Written over and over again, over his own writings, his own thoughts.

'HomeHomeHomeHomeHomeHomeHomeHomeHomeHome HomeHomeHomeHomeHomeHomeHomeHomeHomeHomeH omeHomeHomeHome'

Tom threw the notebook across the room like a snake about to bite him. He put his head in his hands. He tried to think, but he couldn't find anything to make sense of what had just happened. The wiring, the dog, and now this? Tom tried to speak, tried to say something that would make sense of it all. The room seemed that little darker, that little tighter, like the night had grown teeth. Hungry ghosts lurking in the darkness of the walls, waiting for someone to stray that little bit too far.

"I'm losing my fucking mind." He saw something move on the monitor. He turned his head, his neck creaking and popping. Standing in the main warehouse in the darkness, a few metres from his office. A figure draped in shadow looking up at the camera.

20
Shadows With Teeth

Tom eyed the spectre on the camera. His body went tight, gripping his baseball bat. He watched the figure cross the threshold into the office. Tom could hear the footsteps from behind the door. The figure on the monitor standing still at the foot of the SEC RITY room. He tried to call out, but the vice of fear clenched around his neck like a stranglehold of an MMA fighter. He sat there, waiting. The air still, his heart pounding in his ears, his breath deep. The handle of the door began to rattle. Tom struggled to his feet, standing with the bat primed like a baseball player ready to score the big win. His leg ached and yearned for release, it shaking, trying not to buckle as his muscles burned. Tom forced the pain to the back of his mind. The handle turned once more, and the SEC RITY room door pushed open.

The torch was blinding and Tom put his hand over his eyes. "Come any closer and I'll bash your fucking skull in!"

"Hey, hey no need for that now," a voice said. "I'm here to check the alarm." Tom felt the fear drain from him.

"You are?"

"Yeah," the torch holder said. "You the Nightman?" Tom nodded.

"Hey, you mind lowering that damn light? Fuckin blinding me over here."

"Oh, sorry," the figure said, lowering the torch. Tom lowered his hand and let his eyes adjust once more to the night. He sat back down on his chair, putting the bat across his lap. "I didn't mean to startle ya," the figure said, his accent a mix of American and Northern English. "I tried to call the office line but no one answered so I had to make my way here. Everything good?" Tom thought of that question.

"Everything is fine," he said. "I got locked out before and had to break my way in. That's what set the alarm off. Everything's fine though," Tom said with a resounding sigh. The figure nodded his head. He was tall, real fucking tall, maybe around six-eight, six-nine, no hair on top and as thin as a coat hanger. Tom thought he had a slight resemblance to Jack Skellington. "Hey," Tom began.

"Yeah?"

"You didn't happen too..." *Write in my notebook did you? Tell me I'm not going crazy.* "Come by earlier on? We speak before?" The tall man's face contorted; his greyed features dull in the light of the monitors.

"No," he said flatly. "No this is the first time I have been here in a few months."

"Oh," Tom resounded, more confused than before. "I spoke to someone outside when I was locked out. I thought that might have been you." The tall man shook his head.

"No," he repeated. "Not been here in a few months." Tom felt something off about the guy, a little unnerved.

"Well, thanks for checking in," Tom said, turning away from the guy and going back to the monitors. He checked the time and confusion slapped him once more. It was still three AM. But that was impossible? He had been back in the SEC RITY room for at least twenty minutes. Was there a problem with the computers? *Great,* he thought. "Listen man I'm not being rude, but I just wanna get my night done with. So if you don't mind?" Tom began flicking through the monitors, waiting for a response, for the sound of the door closing. But it never came. Tom noticed something on the monitors. The car park. Only his car was there. He sat back, that icy chill slowly filling his stomach once more. "Say," he said, trying to hide the shaking in his voice. "How did you get here?" No response. Tom clenched his eyes shut, then with every part of him screaming not to look, he opened his eyes once more and turned the chair around. The tall man was still standing there, his face etched in a long grin.

"I walked," he said, his fingers clicking together.

"You walked?" Tom said, gripping the handle of the bat once more. The tall man's eyes fixated on the bat. His smile widened.

"Yes," he said, "From the woods." Tom felt the horror firmly cup his balls and squeeze. "Did you like my book? I left it for you. Have you seen my dog?"

"What the fuck did you say?" Tom stammered.

"Are you going to give me a gift like the last one?"

"The last one? A fucking gift?" The tall man nodded.

"Yes. My home. You're in my home. The last one gave his blood. What will you give?" Tom stared at the spectre in stunned terror. *The last one? Walter? Wallace? He heard Jerry's voice in his head -*
'He was a weird guy. Was still alive too when the cleaner found him. Taken away in the ambulance. Kept on talking about 'The Night.''

Tom stood once more, finding the bravery that had been trodden on by the dark, pulling it back into his heart. He held the bat by his shoulder, ready to knock this weird fuck's head off if he took a step his way.

"Get the fuck out of here right now," Tom spat. "Go on! Beat it!" The tall man smiled once more.

"The Grey Man will come for you," he said. "The Grey Man knows your fears. Your past. He will take you soon." The figure rushed to Tom, howling, screaming, long arms outstretched. Tom swung the bat, the head of destruction cutting through the air. He lost his balance, cascading to the floor near the tables of the coffee machine. The carpet licking his cheeks. His breath was ragged, sweat pouring out of his flesh, his leg screaming in hot agony. Tom turned, expecting to see the creature over him, but he was alone once more. He turned again and faced the darkness under the table. He heard breathing coming from under there. *Ghosts with teeth waiting for someone to stray too far.* Tom remembered the torch in his pocket. He licked his lips, the breathing, panting, coming from under the desk growing louder. *The dog?* He wondered. *Have you seen my dog?* He pulled out the torch and clicked it to life. The beam pierced his dead eyes first. His mouth was stretched in a scream. His beard frosted over. The yellow and grey Kevlar overalls covered in seaweed.

Tom dropped the torch, as Brad's swollen face stretched into a toothless grin.

21
Some Things Should Stay Buried.

Tom bolted back to the other side of the room, his leg erupting in agony, the bandages coming away, reopening the wound. He stared in horror at the blackness. The torch still in his hand shaking furiously. He wanted to scream, but his voice couldn't find the air. He shook his head in fury. *It's not real. It's not real.* He knew he shouldn't. He knew he wouldn't. He knew he couldn't. But he knew he would. He bit down on his fear and lowered the bright beam of light to the lip of the table above, and then in one quick flash, the torch found under the base once more.

Brad's smile was stretched from ear to ear. A long toothless grin that fixated on Tom. His eyes met the dead holes in Brad's head.

You left me. He heard the corpse whisper, lips not moving. That grin waxy. Holding itself. *You left me alone on that rig. The black tides pulled me under, as you went to get another bottle from your cabin.* Tom's mind fractured. He didn't want to blink, fearing what he would see when his eyes reopened, but the clicking and popping of those dead bones forced him to focus on that pale bloated skin. The impossible in front of him.

"I...," he started. "I didn't..." He felt his eyes begin to well. "I didn't leave you. It was an accident."

Liar. The word stretch like nails on a blackboard. *You left me on there to man the rig. Tides were high. Never leave someone alone on the rig at night.*

"I wasn't gone long," Tom pleaded. "I was gone only a minute."

Liiiiieeees. The mound spoke. *You left me. You were drunk, and wanted more. I called for help when the tide got too rough. Then the black swallowed me up.* Tom remembered hearing the sounds of screaming, the siren blaring. The flashing of red in his blurred vision as the rig rocked, or his drunken legs shook him as he clambered onto the deck. The rest of the crew throwing life rings over board. Spotlights shining over the pelting rain into the deathly black abyss. The sight of a man taking lung fulls of saltwater, his head vanishing under the waves.

I'm still down there, Brad hissed. *In the black. Fat and swollen, my eyes eaten by hungry fish.*

"You're not real," Tom cried, the torch heavy in his hands. The light begin to flicker, splutter and die. Tom saw Brad's face vanish into the darkness once more. He felt the wind in his ears. The taste of salt on his lips. The monitor went dead. Tom sat silently in the darkness. The beating of his heart in his head. The sound of shuffling. Wet heavy footsteps on the floor. The sound of dripping. Sliding. Getting closer. Tom held his breath. The torch came back to life. He was above him now. And he found his voice in a scream as the icy fingertips wrapped around his throat.

22
Dead Men

Tom fumbled and screamed as the grip of Brad's fingers squoze around his throat. He could feel the air of the Atlantic hitting his face. The deafening sound of the sirens in his ears. The taste of sea salt on his tongue. *You left me, you left me, you left me* the corpse's voice bounced around Tom's mind over and over. *It should have been you, you drunk! You criminal! You waste! It should have been you!* Tom felt shells and rotten fish fall onto his face, Brad's withered face cast in shadow from the shaking torch. His nose missing, the torch light pushing through the holes in his face. Tom squoze his eyes shut, the sound of the tide ravaging him, the feeling of water consuming him, he thrashed, his arms and fingers gliding through black heavy sea. He tried to breathe but a mouthful of salt water forced its way into his lungs. He saw the torch lights blurred and hazy above him as he sank deeper into the Atlantic, before all light vanished, and he was left sinking in the consuming depths.

Tom heaved gulps of air, turning on his front, the taste of salt water lacing his tongue, his nose and eyes stinging. He forced himself onto all fours, coughing until his lungs felt that they were going to give out, spewing bile and retching until nothing more came. As quickly as it had come, it was no more. Tom reluctantly opened his eyes, his face sweating. His breath fast and shallow, whimpering quietly to himself. He was alone. The security monitors still blinking as they always were, switching camera lenses from the white out of the car park, the dead space in the offices, and the empty warehouse. The torch was by his feet, solid light beam engaged.

Tom took hold of the torch and shakily checked the shadows for monsters, but he found none there. Brad was gone. The depths of the abyss vanished. The feeling of weightlessness and water a memory that lingered in his mind, if it had ever been there in the first place. He tried not to think, but he was exhausted, his mind redlining so fierce it had broken, the cogs and pistons from the engine had come loose. He got to his feet, grabbed his bag, and stumbled for the exit. He stopped. He needed his pass to get out of the car park otherwise it was a long fucking walk home. He reluctantly moved back to the monitors and flicked through. The Doberman was in the cafeteria sleeping on one of the couches, his pass still wrapped around its leg. *Have you seen my dog?* The voice in his head crept in once more. Tom told it to *fuck off,* no longer giving himself to the fucking delusions of his own mind. *I'm going insane,* he thought once more, and that, somehow, was more comforting than the alternative.

Tom put his bag down and pulled out some small chicken bites. He couldn't remember what food tasted like. The touch of water on a dry throat a distant memory. He noticed his hands were shaking. He wanted a drink of Vodka so badly.

The warehouse was deathly silent as he stepped out from the SEC RITY room. He could see his breath in front of him, a gust of ghostly mist leaving his mouth. He began to shiver and wrapped his jacket tight around him. The metal walls of the warehouse creaked and groaned as the winter wind ran through them like an uninvited guest. Tom moved through the corridor, shining the torch into the corners, waiting to see those dead eyes once more. In front of him, the light from the cafeteria spilled through onto the floor. He could hear the soft snoring of the dog, and Tom took his bat out of his bag. His leg was hurting badly, and he could feel the warmth leaking out of him, his trousers sticking into him with each step. Tom flicked off the torch and placed it in his bag and gripped the bat with both hands. He turned into the cafeteria, and the bat fell from his grip, rattling on the floor.

He stumbled as his legs went weak and caught himself on the counter. The room had transformed. It wasn't the cafeteria anymore. The blue couches had disappeared. The busted TV and coffee machine no longer there. The room wasn't brightly lit with harsh strip lighting. It was dim, the smell of bleach pushing up his nose. The sight of her, lying there, tubes coming out of her arms, face and stomach. The machine she was strapped too keeping her breathing as the dull bedside lamp flickered on her hospital bed.

"Jayne?"

23
Closer

His throat swelled and finally, the tears pushed through. His hands and knees met the vinyl flooring as he crawled to her bed. The itchy blue blanket crumpling in his fists as he clambered to her. The steel bed frame met his palms. His face met hers. His eyes searching for something, anything that would make sense. He could smell her. He could touch her. He could feel her warmth on his fingertips as he held her face.

He tried to speak but he couldn't. He wouldn't. Nothing he could say would bring her back. Nothing he could do would make her wake up. Just like that day when he got home from the rig. When she had been lying there in the hospital. He climbed on the bed and it creaked and yearned under his weight. He lay next to her. His eyes burning, his cheeks red. The touch of her hair through his fingers. She was here but so far away. A skeleton wrapped in withered skin. He fell into that space he didn't want to visit. That place of despair, when all has crumbled around you, and you can't find the strength to pick up the pieces.

Tom went to speak, to say something. That he loved her. That he missed her. That he was sorry he wasn't there for her. That he leaned on her too much when he got back, about his drinking, his past. All the bad shit he had done and she had given him nothing but unconditional love in return. That he was sorry she couldn't come home. He told her about the day they first met. A friend's birthday party. The blue dress she had worn and he pointed out she had spilt cream from the buffet on the cuff. They laughed and she put the stray dab on his lips before taking it with her own.

How he had touched her and held her that night as they made love. When two became one, and he had been a part of her ever since, and she him.

"I'm sorry," he whispered finally. His despair bleeding into his words like paint mixing together on a soiled carpet. "Wake up baby," he cried, stroking her face. "Wake up baby." Tom closed his eyes and held her hand in his, falling into her embrace.

24
Little By Little

Tom opened his eyes and saw his wife gone. He was on the ground, his arms stretched out onto the floor, his face on the cold flooring of the cafeteria room. He felt fur brushing his face, and then the cold of a snout. The room was how it had been, his wife no longer here. A projection of his own fear. The Doberman sitting next to him, the pass around his paw, its tongue long and pink panting away, drooling on the floor. Rage gripped him then. He lunged at the animal, it recoiling from him, baring its teeth. The dog snapped those hellish jaws to him, its teeth burying into his leather jacket. He felt the power of its jaws as it latched on. Tom howled at the beast to let him go, to fuck off back into the cold. The dog thrashed and its teeth tore through his jacket sleeve and found the cold skin underneath. He smelt the potent sharp odor of blood permeating the air. Tom reeled his hand back and punched the mutt in the snout. It didn't release, he punched it again, the pain of the night, of what he had seen, his misery coming to the forefront. The other shit of the night might have been his own head playing tricks, but this dog was real. He punched it one last time and the animal moved backwards, nestling behind the blue sofa. Tom snatched at the Doberman's back paw, unlooping the tangled lanyard of his ID and stuffed it into his pocket. He stepped back quickly, less the dog want another go of him. His arm erupted in agony, the blood flowing freely, dripping on his pants and the ground like a painter with too much liquid on the brush and too far from the canvas.

Tom turned and moved for the corridor, lanyard in hand, and the smell of freedom permeating the air. He hobbled through the dark corridor, his leg shaking, his arm bleeding, his car keys firmly in his hand, his bat and duffel bag over his back.

Outside the double glass doors, he saw his truck sitting there, encased in thick ice. He pushed the release button on the wall. A flickering red light met his eye. His heart plummeted. He pushed it again. Still nothing. The doors didn't budge. He hammered the button over and over, trying to hold back the panic which sat on his shoulder like a hungry vulture. He dropped his back to the ground and took out the bat. He swung that motherfucker as hard as he could against the glass, the head of bat bouncing back, sending a violent tremor through Tom's wrist and shoulder. He dropped the bat to the floor where it rattled on the ground. Tom eyed the bullseye in the glass, and then, before his eyes, it reformed into a flawless, smooth surface. Tom moved to the glass and put his hand to it. From the bottom of his lungs came the scream he had been holding back all night. He thrashed and bashed at the glass. "Let me out! Let me the fuck out!" He picked up the bat once more and went hell for leather, each time the bat bouncing off the glass, the bullseyes reforming, and the tremors racing up Tom's shoulder.

"Sash?" The sound struck him like a truck blindsiding a soccer mom with too much gin in her system for a Sunday morning. Jayne was standing there, looking as beautiful as she did the first day they had met. The thought of her in the hospital bed.

"You're not here," he said through gritted teeth, tears gathering on his lip. She moved to him, and he felt her warm touch on his face. She dressed to his front, those green eyes piercing his through the night. She touched his lips with hers, running her hand through the back of his hair.

"I'm here baby," Jayne said. "I'm here. I won't leave you to face this alone. We need to stay here; you won't make it back to the hospital in the state you're in. You won't make it baby."

"I have to get back to you," Tom said. "I need to get back to you, make sure you're okay." She smiled, that same smile that always melted the worry from his heart, that smile that pierced through his most stubborn moments, her face soft, melting away the ice in his heart.

"I'm here," she whispered. She kissed him once more and he held her tightly. "I want you to stay with me Sash, stay here with me. Don't leave me alone in the dark." Tom tried to think of what to say, what reasoning for what was happening. The lights in the foyer came to life and the hallway lit up in bright, warm light. "Come on baby," Jayne whispered again, holding his face in both hands. Stay here with me forever."

25
Jerry

Jerry scratched his stomach as he hauled himself up and sat on the corner of his bed. His phone had lit up and a notification stared at him. He picked it up and read that the alarm had been activated at Welch Mill. Jerry felt the dread creep along his skin. He took out a cigarette from the pack by his bedside and lit it, letting the thick smoke fill his lungs as he dialled the number for work. The call didn't connect. He tried once more and still nothing. He rubbed his eyes and checked the time. Nearly 4 am. Memories plagued him of Wallace, and he felt worry enter his heart as he got out of bed and threw on some clothes.

He was downstairs and had his shoes and coat on within five minutes. This wasn't supposed to happen. Not Tom. He wasn't like the others; the dark couldn't take him. Not like the others. Not like the murderers and other convicts he had given to the night. Tom wasn't like that, but death knows no morality of men. We are all worm food in the end. Jerry moved through the house and caught a glimpse of a photo. There, in six by nine, a picture of his daughter before they had gone to the beach. The last photo he would ever take of her. He would have her back again soon, but the long nights of insomnia, drinking himself to sleep, his body and mind destroying at the price he had to pay. He couldn't do it anymore. He had to make it stop.

Jerry walked out and the cool winter air bit his skin. In his car he put the heating on and brushed the gathered snow from his windscreen. It was still falling, and he hoped the roads were clear and he could get there before it was too late.

He reversed out the driveway and took off down the long empty streets, streetlights gliding over him as he drew closer. He saw the sign for Downtown and took the exit of the freeway, his thoughts running around his head.

Jerry checked his pockets to make sure he had everything he needed. He needed to be more prepared this time. After the last guy had called him in the middle of the night, there wasn't much left of him by the time he got there. He touched his coat pockets. He had his cigarettes. His phone. His wallet, and more importantly, his gun.

His heart was in pieces since the first day Tom had walked through the front doors of the building. He had a record, yes, but he wasn't a bad man. Not like the others he had offered. Not like the others at all. *It wasn't time* Jerry thought. *It's not supposed to happen yet.* He wasn't like the others. He wasn't like the other pieces of shit that worked the night shift: ex-convicts, drug users, killers. The kind of people they would normally hire to do the night shift. The one which the entity wanted. Those that could have *accidents* on sight. Those who society wouldn't miss. Those who had more darkness in their hearts than good. Tom wasn't like them. He should have never given him the job. He passed the interview; Carl was sure about that. He was a candidate, no one would ask questions if he got a little squirrely with what he had been through. But he couldn't do it. Three nights was far too much for him. Normally the Mill would be more gentle, eroding them slower. But it appeared that was happening much faster this time. More aggressive. The shadows with teeth.

"When death asks why?" He whispered to himself as he drove down the snowy highway. "When death asks why."

Jerry arrived at the Mill around fifteen minutes later. He checked his watch. He still had some time left. He needed to get Tom out. He needed to stop this thing once and for all. He pulled up to the pick-up truck Tom had left to be devoured by ice. He killed the engine and stepped out of his Sedan. His boots crunching under his feet as he moved to the entrance of the building. He shone his torch through the dark glass. A baseball bat and spats of dried blood on the carpet. His mouth turned dry. He hoped he wasn't too late to save him. He lifted his ID to the door to open it, but the doors came open freely, the darkness welcoming him inside. He took a deep breath, took the pistol out from his coat, and stepped into the foyer, the doors closing behind him.

26
The Dark

Jerry eyed the bat on the floor and the lanyard discarded next to it. *He nearly got away,* Jerry thought, remembering the last time this had happened. The sound of Gretta's teeth crunching around the poor bastards' fingers. Jerry finding him lying on the ground in a pool of his own blood. Then glimpsing the hounds' eyes as it slunk away into the warehouse racking's, drips of blood dotting from its long pink tongue.

Jerry crossed the threshold into the hell mouth, smelling the sodden carpet and the fresh potpourri left out on the counter. He heard the sound of growling coming from behind him. He ignored the rod of ice creeping up his spine. He knew better than to look the death hound in the eyes.

The pistol in his hand, Jerry stalked slowly through the hallway. It was dark, but luckily he brought a torch. All the lights were off in the warehouse. Not even the cafeteria light was on anymore, and that damn thing was *never* off. Jerry liked to keep it that way, like some kind of safe haven. Monsters don't like the light. That's why it's always safe to stay away from the shadows. That's why he hated staying here too late.

It was silent at first, only the sound of Jerry's heavy breathing pushing through the black. *Tom could be anywhere* he wondered. He touched the door handle of the HR office. He pulled down slowly and the door released with a reluctant *click.* It was dead inside. Only two empty desks with black monitors. Nothing of concern. The door closed too and Jerry continued to walk towards the main hall.

Again, the sound of growling behind him. Closer this time. So close, he could feel the dog's hot panting on the back of his jeans. Jerry didn't turn around. He knew what would happen if he looked that thing in the eyes. Those big brown spheres of the death hound. The evil this place holds. Like staring into the heart of a murderer. Nothing good will come of it. Two more heavy steps and Jerry swallowed dryly. The sound of a whimper behind him. He passed the door of Management, his own office. Maybe Tom had taken some sort of solace inside there? He had tried to call him, however, now he thought about it he wasn't sure it had been Tom calling him or it was the being that fed from him inside this place. Jerry didn't believe in ghosts, but he did believe in evil. This place wasn't haunted. He hadn't ever seen a ghost or a spirit, no poltergeist throwing toilet paper or hiding people's car keys. But something did live in these woods and the surrounding area, and he had seen that with his own eyes, the day his daughter died. Like it fed off his grief, and offered him a way back from it.

The hound was in front of him. Those eyes dark pits of death. The tongue pale and flat. Its lips crumpled, teeth coming out to play. Jerry averted his gaze, putting his hand to his face. His heart jackhammered and he felt icy rain wash over him. The hound moved closer. It pawed at his leg and its snout nestled his pockets and licked at his coat. Jerry tried not too look, like a child watching someone butchering a rabbit at a magic show. They know they shouldn't watch, but they just can't help it. We are drawn to the things that wish to damage us the most.

The hound stood up on its hind legs. It was nearly as tall as him. Jerry pushed back into the wall, tried to catch himself but fell backwards. The hound was over him low, licking at those tightly closed eyes. Jerry could feel its bare rib cage against his fingertips, the flesh dangling from its insides. The gun in his pocket being squoze harder than a desperate virgin's dick who just discovered online porn. Its nose was cold, touching Jerry's reddening cheeks. He tried not to breathe, the stench of rot making him gag. That, and it was the only way he could hold back the scream that wanted to burst from his lungs.

The hound sat back, panting heavily on his face. It growled again, and Jerry wanted so badly to shoot the thing in between the eyes. But if he did that, the creature would have him. He would be inviting it in. Inviting it to hurt him, to ravage him. Jerry could only wait. Wait until the torment was over. Resist the urge to look into that hollow skull that still moved. Those empty eye sockets. The thing that should have died but still wandered the halls of this place.

The creature leaned in and barked. Spittle flying into Jerry's face. He squoze his eyes tighter, the grip on the gun turning his knuckles white. He heard the sound of shouting coming from the warehouse. The sound of a man screaming, wailing and begging. His eye lids snapped open and sweat bled into his eyes making them rampage like dipped in lemon juice. He eyed the doorway. It was open, light spilling through the dark corridor. The glow of the emergency lighting in the warehouse casting the shelving and desks in a dull red, reminding Jerry of the old dark rooms of photo production.

He could feel the hound's snout on his cheek. The brush of its teeth on his face. He closed his eyes again just as the jaws of death opened wide to sink its teeth into his flesh.

27

Bargaining

Jerry pushed the beast off him. He crawled to his feet. He stumbled and caught himself on the wall. He turned and saw the hell hound gone. The keeper of the gate. The bringer of souls. Jerry pushed harder, reaching the door to the warehouse where Tom was. He grabbed the handle but it was burning hot. He pulled his hand back, the handle steaming into the night air. He looked around him, hoping to see an answer, maybe to see God staring back at him? Or even the Devil himself…

"Haven't you had enough!" He screamed to the encroaching blackness. "Haven't I given you enough!"

I gave you your daughter back the voice bled from the black. *You have a debt to be paid. You have a debt to fill.*

"I have given you many!" He screamed, tears of pain flowing freely, his teeth bared.

I desire one more. I desire this one. The voice called again, swirling around Jerry's ears. *I require one more to take. One more to feed. Why do you care about this one?*

"Because I can't live like this!" He screamed. "I can't go on living like this! He isn't like the others, he has a wife, she needs him. He isn't like the others! He has done wrong but he is not a bad man, he has demons like all of us!" The darkness paused, then, the sinister voice filled his mind once more.

One more soul, or I will take her back. A light in the foyer flickered then died. A figure, small and thin, approached him. A silhouette with short cut hair. A tube through her nose. A small stuffed bear in her hand, as she moved towards him. The light blinked, and she was closer. Step by step, closer and closer, limbs popping, arms and knees dislocated, crunching and warped as she moved. The light flickered out, and black surrounded him. One last snatch of a glimpse through the etched window and he could see Tom on his knees, the entity before him. The dog by its side, and the tall man with it. He turned one last time. His daughter, what *looked* like his daughter, was standing behind him, her eyes sunken to the back of her head, her cheeks eroded, maggots falling from the fleshy black wound.

Daddy…

Jerry took out the gun from his pocket and kicked at the door until it blasted open and bolted through the entrance.

28
Headrush

Jerry raced through the door which exploded in a barrage of twisted steel and flying wood. He raised the gun, screaming at Tom, screaming at him to move away. He saw the entity touching him. The *Grey Man. Its* skin withered, teeth black, hair thin and a soiled cloth that wrapped around its emaciated body. It was leaning over Tom, drinking him, his soul being devoured in front of his eyes and *The Grey Man* took it hungrily. His mouth wide open, eyes rolled to the back of his head. "No!" Jerry howled. "Not this one! You can't have another one! Enough is enough!"

One more soul or I will take her from you spoke the darkness. Next to the beings, his daughter appeared once more, a white bead of light coming from her chest to the Grey Man's chest. The Tall Man snarled. He touched the thread of light and tightened it between his long, bony fingers. Jerry recoiled.

"No!"

Jerry raised the weapon and took aim at the Tall Man. It reeled its head back, then lunged its long face to him, his eyes pits of black, mouth hanging low as darkness spewed out the wails of hell. The room closed black and shadow fell around him. He was blinded in blackness. Jerry searched the empty void around him, his voice sounding far away, echoing around an empty abyss. He took out his torch, trying to find someone, something, but the beam continued stretching, the cold pricking Jerry's skin. The light stretched and stretched, finding nothing but empty space around him. He called out, and he heard only his voice disappearing in the emptiness faster than he uttered it. He was in *that place* again. The place beyond this world. The place he had seen in the eyes of those he gave to the Grey Man.

I require one more the darkness said. *I require one more. One of darkness. One of pain. I require one more for my collection. I require one more. Only one more, or I will take her from you and bring her back to me.* Jerry searched the darkness more but found nothing.

"You can't have him. I can't do this anymore. I can't feed you more!"

Then I will take her from you the dark said. Jerry screamed in protest, howling for his daughter, howling for mercy. He dropped to his knees, his heart rampaging. The torch fell to the floor. Tom saw the pair of feet in front of him. His daughter standing there. The thread from her chest like a streak of light in the blackness. Her face unmoving. Her skin healed, no longer ridden in maggots or decay.

"Please don't take her from me," Jerry cried. "Please, let him go. Take me instead." With that, the Grey Man appeared in front of Jerry. It reeled in closely, touching his face. Its teeth were tombstones of black and yellow, tongue and gums eroded and blackened. Its nose curved, face wrinkled, skin grey and yellow, like thin leather draped over bones. It touched a long fingernail to its chest, and from it, a thread of light followed. The Grey Man hovered its finger over Jerry's chest.

"When death asks you why?" It said, its breath like decayed meat.

"I can't live with myself anymore. What kind of monster am I? I have taken so many. Given you so many."

"Deservedly of the fate they suffered," it spoke. Jerry shook his head.

"I was desperate. I did anything I could to bring her back, but I can't do this any longer. I can't give you another. Not this one." Jerry saw Tom lying on the ground beside the Grey Man, a thread of light from his chest leading into the creatures. He thought of his daughter once more, tears falling onto the ground. "If you're not breathing… why am I?"

"We had a deal," the creature spoke. "Your daughter's life for one day a year, for the lives of the damaged." It lingered its fingertip over Jerry's chest once more. "When death asks you why?" Jerry felt the answer burning in his throat. The same question the Grey Man always asked. The same question it always asked before it took someone. Before it gave him his daughter back in return for a soul. He put the torch once more to his daughter's face. She was perfect, the tubing from her nose now gone. Her bones no longer broken from the car accident. "When death asks you why…" The Grey Man said, pointing to the black. Jerry followed the darkness and shone his torch.

Seven. Seven in total standing there. Each driven mad by the darkness as an offering to it, until it consumed them. One with a chewed-up hand. *Wallace.* The rapist. A woman with a ligature mark on her neck. She had done it in the bathroom. The thief. Another, a faceless man holding a torch, blood leaking from his skull and barbed wire tearing into his legs as he tried to climb the fencing to escape. The drug dealer. A woman screaming, banging on the walls of the elevator who had suffocated. The fraudster. A man in his thirties frozen to death. The violent. The Tall Man, the first of them, who was lost in the forest in a blizzard, finding the Welch Mill with his hound, begging Jerry for shelter but was met with a box cutter to the stomach instead. Standing there, their heads facing the floor. Their eyes closed. "When death asks you why…" The Grey man said once more. His daughter moved to him, the bear in her hand. Her small digits wrapping around his neck, holding him tightly.

"Because I love her," Jerry said, squeezing her tightly in his big arms. The Grey Man lifted his head. Jerry stood and moved to him. He held out his hand and he understood. He cast his eyes on the blackness, on the hound, on the victims of his cruel creation. He stared into the eyes of his daughter who held out the pistol. The Grey Man touched his chest, the string of light complete. Jerry put the gun to his temple, and the darkness consumed him.

28
Cycle

Tom awoke on the floor of the foyer to the feeling of someone slapping his face. He opened his eyes and saw the morning cleaner, a tanned lady with fake lips as plump as bee stings, scalded him.

"Get up!" She howled. "Get up now! What's the matter with you? I've been knocking for thirty minutes! I'm late to work now! Get up before the boss gets here!" Tom sat up, his body ached. He turned to see the morning sun breaking through the thick clouds above. He got to his feet and checked himself over. The wound to his leg had gone, and so had the bite on his arm. He stared at himself, checking his clothing and his body intently, like he had woken up from a surgery with a pair of breasts when he went under for a root canal.

"I'm okay?" He said, astonished. The cleaner held him with contempt.

"You night workers are all fucking weirdos. I think it's the dark. Drives you all crazy." Tom didn't care, he stretched out his body and let the pops and clicks come. He hadn't felt this great in a long time, his first real night's sleep. He tried to remember what had happened, how he had gotten to the foyer? But as much as he tried, he couldn't quite snatch the memory from his mind, like trying to grab fleeting smoke. "So go on," the cleaner said, her arms folded. "What did you go to jail for? That's all they hire here for your job. Convicts, weirdos. You're on camera so don't try anything. I do Krav Maga." Tom scrunched his face and let out the biggest laugh he has in a long time.

"I'm going home back to my wife," he said as he exited the foyer. "Fuck this place." Tom walked along the icy tarmac to his truck. He de-iced the windscreen and cracked the door open. He turned the ignition on and let the car warm up and demist. Getting into the driver's seat, he cranked it in reverse and pulled out of the car park. He couldn't wait to see his wife, to tell her he had quit, that he was leaving that place for good.

As he drove steadily down the long country highway, he tapped the steering wheel to his favourite song that played on the radio, him singing at the top of his lungs. He didn't see them watching him as he moved away through the trees, or the Doberman that crossed the road behind him, looking for its next meal. Eight of them. Eight in total. Waiting for the next person to take over the Night Shift.

About the author

Jay Darkmoore lives in the Northwest of England and is a huge fan of all things dark - exploring the macabre, demonic and darker aspects of the human psyche.

Jay likes putting his characters in terrible situations and then turning out all the lights. To date, he has self-published novels of horror, dark fantasy dystopia, as well as horror shorts compilations.

When not at his desk, Jay spends his free time making YouTube videos to help writers in their craft, promoting other books he has enjoyed, as well as hitting the gym and taking wild cold plunges with ducks.

He is a single parent to his son Joe who is his biggest fan.

If you enjoyed this title, please leave a review. Reviews are how indie authors make a name for themselves and are able to keep releasing content for you hungry readers to eat up.

Thank you for taking the time and spending it reading my work. I thoroughly hoped you enjoyed it. If you would like to see more of my work, look below –

For my books, head to Amazon Kindle Store and search 'Jay Darkmoore.'

For my website, blog and mailing list of exclusive content, head to www.Jaydarkmooreauthor.com

For my socials, head to Instagram Jay_Darkmoore_Author.

For my YouTube channel of original horror stories found nowhere else, search 'Jay Darkmoore.'

- J

Printed in Great Britain
by Amazon